CAPTURING

A

UNICORN

EVE LANGLAIS

Chimera S

Copyright © 2018/19, Eve Langlais

Cover Dreams2Media © 2018/19

Produced in Canada

Published by Eve Langlais ~ www.EveLanglais.com

eBook ISBN: 978 1 77 384 09 01

Print ISBN: 978 1 77 384 09 18

PROLOGUE

THE SLEEPING DRUG WORE OFF AND EMMA AWOKE in a helicopter. Which wasn't exactly a normal kind of thing for her.

Most times, she woke in a bed with a pillow under her head. On a few rare occasions, she woke up on the floor, cold and wet, as if doused while she slept. Her clothes missing. The faint hint of copper, the tangy blood kind, hanging in the air. Her head shorn down to the scalp.

Despite the heavy drugged feeling, she didn't smell violence—only a bit of body odor not her own—garlic from a meal too heavily doused with it, and oil, the kind that permeated machines that received regular maintenance.

The chopper was airborne. It vibrated and made a hellishly loud noise, and she didn't wear anything to muffle it. Bare ears didn't mean she heard much. No one spoke; however, she got the impression she wasn't alone.

Emma kept her head ducked while she gauged the situation. It helped that her hair hung in her face, hiding any tics that might have given away the fact she was awake. She'd prefer not to get jabbed with a needle or gassed—again. Especially since she had no idea what had happened.

Where are they taking me?

Last thing Emma recalled, she was reading in her room—a decent-sized space with a bed, television, and her own bathroom. She was one of the luckier patients. Or, as Dr. Sphinx used to tell her, "You're a good girl, Emma." And good girls got treats. For example, a well-behaved patient might be rewarded with a decent room and amenities—like hot water and coconut pudding pie.

What of the bad ones, the patients who just loved to rebel against authority? Those that survived their illness and treatment and got temperamental about their second lease on life got to live in tiny cells and eat flavorless gruel. Or so Emma had heard via the grapevine. She never saw or experienced it herself. Emma wasn't the type to rock her comfy boat.

Which begged the question, why did they knock her out and decide to move her? It wasn't just Dr. Sphinx that reassured her she would always have a home at the Chimaeram Clinic. Dr. Chimera himself, the man who saved her life, promised she didn't ever have to go anywhere. *"You can stay here as long as you need, Emma. We're your family now."*

What had changed? Did this have to do with the sirens? The strident shriek of warning, abrupt and much too loud, had sent Emma to her knees, hands over her ears, rocking at the pain of it. Shaking in terror. She didn't handle change very well. Didn't handle much well at all.

Her life seemed to be a never-ending symphony of tragedies. She didn't want to be a perpetual victim, but bad things kept happening to her.

The blaring siren ended as abruptly as it began. No warning. No explanation provided via the speaker in her ceiling. As a matter of fact, not a single person came by to tell Emma what was happening. Then again, why would they? She was simply a patient on level five who chose to remain hidden from the world.

Probably the only patient of Dr. Chimera's that welcomed the lock on her door. Locks kept out the monsters that liked to creep in the dead of night, place their hands over a mouth, and whisper, *"Stay still and this won't hurt."*

What a lie that was. But for a long time, she believed it, accepted the abuse as her due. The psychiatrist who treated her in the clinic taught her to accept that nothing in her past was her fault. That she could control her future.

If that were the case, then why did she sit in a helicopter, flitting away from the place she called home?

They could have asked me if I wanted to go. They didn't have to drug her.

Unless it was an emergency and they didn't have time. Maybe related to the sirens. Could be a mass evacuation. Still, they could have warned her before filling her room with gas.

She must have hit the floor hard because her jaw ached. But she knew it wouldn't last long. Injuries rarely concerned her anymore. Such a change from a few years ago.

I used to bruise easily as a peach. The mottled patches on her skin a rainbow of color in varying degrees. Or, as Tommy used to say, *"You're like a canvas for my fists."* And he liked painting. It was a relief when they threw him in jail for robbing a gas station.

The sad part was her next boyfriend didn't prove any better. But that was a long time ago. The bruises were gone now, and they wouldn't be coming back. The clinic kept her safe. Hid her from a cruel world.

And she wasn't the only one.

She heard a grunt amidst the chopper noise and almost lifted her head to peek. In the interest of feigning sleep while she gauged the situation, she chose to glance through the hunks of hair falling in her face.

Across from Emma sat another patient. A man, not one she'd ever met. Not exactly surprising since she only ever saw the nurses who checked on her, the occasional guard, and the doctors—which was how she liked it since her unfortunate side effect to the therapy.

I don't want anyone to see me like this. To stare at her and point. Some would surely mock. Others might pity. What they would never understand was she welcomed the change in her body because it was the price she paid to live. Enjoying a long pain-free life, even a quiet, secluded one, was preferable to the alternative.

Besides, Dr. Sphinx had assured her that Dr. Chimera was working hard to reverse her deformity. Not that she was in a rush. She would prefer to never leave the clinic. She'd never had it so easy. So good. Three meals a day. A bed. A hot shower, and no one raising a fist if she said no.

She'd suffer a hundred more side effects if it meant being safe.

The man across from her uttered another noise, and she glanced surreptitiously again. Noticed how his chest heaved underneath the pale green smock he wore with matching pants. The garb of a patient. Doctors always wore slacks with a button shirt and tie, white coat layered over top. Nurses wore funny little caps with a red cross in the middle. Guards wore black.

As a patient, yet a special one, Emma wore a pink tracksuit. The big wooly sweater in rainbow colors tucked around her, a present from Dr. Sphinx.

A subtle wiggle on her toes showed someone had placed socks on her feet, which was nice. Nothing worse than cold toes. Especially on concrete. It was why Sphinx had a carpet bought for her. Bright pink and shaggy. She loved curling her toes in the texture.

Would she ever see that rug again?

"Whazz happening?" slurred the fellow across from her.

"Sssshhh." The whispered suggestion from her left held a sibilant hiss.

Her head twitched as she shifted to look, only to freeze as the man next to her muttered, "Don't move."

The very fact he noticed halted all further motion.

Awareness prickled her skin. Warned her of danger. It hung in the air, a promise of impending violence.

The man across from her must have felt it, because his agitation grew. "They promised no more chains. Said they'd leave me alone. Let me go." He began to breathe hard. Harsh—*huh, huh, huh*—hot puffs of air.

Funny how hearing it made her own breathing stutter a bit. Panic was contagious.

She kept an eye on the guy, worried about him, especially since his cheeks turned a mottled red. He gazed about with frantic anxiety. She could almost taste his growing panic as he strained at the straps holding him in place. The sturdy canvas wound around his body, the arms encased inside a straight-jacket. A precaution lest the fellow try to escape.

Emma didn't have the same constriction and wore only a regular safety harness. A glance at her lap showed it buckled in the front. She appreciated the trust. Dr. Sphinx knew she'd never try and run.

"Dude, calm down. You don't want them to notice," the guy beside her murmured.

"Fuck you and fuck them," snapped the brutish man, pushing again at the ties holding him.

As feared, it drew attention.

"I told them one dose wasn't enough."

Emma knew that voice. Dr. Sphinx! If he were here, then she knew she'd be all right. She was his special girl. He brought her treats all the time. Not just candy but books, and he made sure she could watch all the newest movies. She regarded him as the benevolent father she never had. The real one left, and then that woman who birthed her had a string of boyfriends. Not all of them were nice. Shoving Darryl down those stairs was worth the two years Emma had to spend in juvenile detention.

But her life was better now. All the Darryls were gone from her life. She had finally reached a Zen place, and Dr. Sphinx was part of that reason.

Emma raised her head and saw his familiar stocky shape standing in the aisle between the jump seats. The military-style chopper didn't possess regular benches. Most of the time, it was used to run big crates of supplies. But it could handle passengers. The walls held fold-down squares of plastic for the butt, not exactly comfortable. Especially if you could not scratch an itchy nose like the guy in front of her.

There were several other patients in the chopper with her. At least five across from her, wearing straitjackets and buckled into their seats. A glance to her left and right showed the same number in her row, along with a few guards. They sat on opposite sides from the cockpit, rifles at the ready. As if they'd shoot in such close confines. But then again, maybe they would if panicked enough. After all, scared people did desperate things.

It was the excuse she gave the judge when asked why she hit Lonny with his own car. It was reversing it over him that got her a year in jail.

Emma knew what fear felt and looked like. She saw it in the nurse who unbuckled from the harness with fumbling hands, knocking her silly white cap with its red cross askew.

Nurse Gretchen—not the nicest of them but not the meanest either—spilled onto her knees and hauled out a chest tucked under her seat. The metal buckles on it snapped, each twang only causing the angry man in front of her to curse louder.

"Fuckingwhorecocksucking—"

The angry words streamed right past her. Emma had learned to filter most profane speech at an early age. She was more interested in the situation around her. Sphinx stood waiting and watching the nurse, whose fear and panic perfumed the air.

It triggered a familiar weakness in Emma that began with trembling limbs and shallow breathing.

Huh-huh-huh.

Not now. She couldn't afford to black out. She glanced elsewhere, noting a few of the patients were awake or no longer faking sleep. There was a woman beside the cursing man, her Asian features smooth, almost ageless, and yet her expression appeared old.

Her eyes pure white. It wouldn't have surprised Emma if she opened her mouth and exhaled a ghostly mist.

On the other side of the angry dude, another body stirred, or so it seemed given the ripple of hair. The very long strands proved lush and thick, covering the owner from head to toe, much like Cousin It in the *Addams Family*.

The nurse offered the ready needle to the doctor.

"Thank you. Prepare a few more, would you. It seems some of our friends have been playing possum."

The angry fellow glared and spat. "Don't you fucking come near me with that thing."

"It will calm you down, Barry."

"I don't want to be fucking calm, asshole. Remove these fucking straps."

Sphinx shook his head. "You know I can't do that. They're for the safety of the passengers on board."

"I'm not a psycho."

"Are you really going to try that lie, Barry?" Sphinx said with a sneer that took her by surprise. "What do you call what happened to that guard?"

The brutish-looking fellow with the deep sloping forehead bared uncharacteristically long sharp teeth in a grin as he said, "I call him delicious. You should try human tartar sometime."

Her stomach heaved as the meaning filtered to her brain. She couldn't stand meat of any kind. Not even a well-cooked burger.

She wasn't the only one disgusted. A woman to her right murmured, "Gross."

"Don't mock it 'til you try it, honey. If you want, I'll save the doctor's heart for you when I tear it from his chest," Barry offered with an evil grin.

"And this is why you should have been left behind with the other irredeemables," Dr. Sphinx muttered.

"What do you mean left behind? What's going on? Where are we going?" asked the man beside her.

"Always asking questions, eh, Jacob?" Sphinx held up the needle and tapped the glass vial. A solid dose of Special Sleeping K. More potent than the darts they used in their guns. More evenly applied than the gas. One prick and the person could be out for days.

"Better asking late than never. You might think we're dumb, but some of us did learn after our shit deal with Lowry." Mr. Lowry being the clinic's lawyer. He usually handled the contract aspect of accepting the clinical trial treatments. Problem being he was a lawyer who used legalese. Most didn't grasp what they signed away.

Emma did. She just didn't care.

"Always whining instead of thankful for the chance you got." Sphinx shook his head, a benevolent father chastising a son—but the cruel hint of mockery around his lips sent a chill down her spine.

"You're dodging instead of answering. What's going on?" asked Jacob.

"Nothing to hide. Count yourselves as the lucky ones. You're ten of less than two dozen we've chosen to keep."

"Keep? We're not things you can own," the woman

to her left with the lightly tanned complexion exclaimed.

"Actually, Janice, according to the terms of your contract, we do. It is up to us to decide if you are fit to be released into the general population again."

"You're the one who isn't fit," spat Janice. "You're a foul excuse for person."

"Insulting the one in charge of your fate." Sphinx tsked. "Not the brightest thing you could do. You really should be nicer to me, Janice."

Emma gaped as she listened. Who was this cold and mean Sphinx? What happened to the father figure she knew?

"Where are we going?" she asked, trying to defuse the situation.

Sphinx glanced her way and offered a warm smile. "Emma, I didn't know you were awake."

"Sorry."

The doctor's smile widened. "Don't be. I'm glad. Maybe you can talk some sense into your seatmates."

"I'm sure they'll be cooperative once we know what's happening. They're just scared." Did their hearts hammer in their chests? Did something inside them stir, something cold and demanding?

A snort blew from Barry. "Scared my ass. More like pissed. This wasn't the deal. None of what they did to me was ever part of the deal."

There were murmurs of agreement from the others.

"The Chimaeram Clinic saved us," Emma reminded them.

"It made me into a bigger prisoner than I was before I lost the use of my legs," snapped Jacob.

"They won't let me talk to my family," Janice huffed.

"What evil was wrought in the deepest parts of the lair shall spill on the world and cause utmost despair." No surprise, the melodic words came from the freaky-eyed lady who still appeared much too calm.

"Keep your prophecies to yourself, Xiu," Sphinx spat.

"Or what?" Xiu, for all her white orbs appeared unseeing, stared in his direction. "You won't punish me. You can't." Her lips split into a wide smile. "Because you'll soon be dead."

For some reason Sphinx appeared quite discomfited by her statement. He glanced at the nurse. "Put her out first before she opens her mouth again."

The nervous nurse took back the needle, and her hand shook as she approached Xiu.

"Leave her alone," shouted Barry, heaving once more at the straightjacket.

"Him next," Sphinx replied rather than rescind the order.

"You're a real piece of work," spat Jacob. "Drugging people who are helpless. Doing unspeakable shit. You need someone to rein you in."

"And who would you suggest oversee our work?"

Sphinx queried. "How does one moderate something experimental?"

The nurse pulled out the depleted needle and went to exchange it for another. Xiu's chin touched her chest, out cold, but Emma found it hard to completely forget what she'd said.

"When I get out of this contraption, I'm coming for you, asshole, and I'm going to make you watch as I eat your lying tongue," growled Barry.

"And you wonder why we had a clause put in the contract that prevents you from walking out our doors." Sphinx shook his head. "It's statements like that that make it impossible for us to declare you cured."

"You never planned to let us go," Janice accused.

In that, Janice was correct. Emma realized early on that, like that line in "Hotel California," checking out just wasn't an option. However, she never cared because the clinic proved to provide a better lifestyle for her.

"What's happening?" asked a new groggy male voice farther down the line.

"Another one awake? Did we screw up the batch of gas?" Sphinx exclaimed. "Fucking animals. I told those idiot techs to triple the dose."

The callous words had her chewing her lower lip. This was so unlike the doctor she knew.

"Was there an emergency?" she dared to ask.

"You might say so. It's why you're being moved to a new, more secure location."

"What happened? Is everyone okay?" she asked,

noting that when Sphinx lifted his arm and the jacket gaped open, there was blood on his shirt.

"No. Nothing is okay." Dr. Sphinx shook his head. "Some cowardly thieves attacked the clinic late afternoon. Many guards were killed."

"Oh no," she gasped.

"Yes!" hissed Barry. "Death to all the clinic staff."

The cruelty drew her gaze. "That's a mean thing to say. They were just people, doing a job."

"A job that involved experimenting on us," Jacob retorted. "Barry's right. I'm also glad they're dead."

"They deserve it," agreed Janice. "I hope those people attack again and kill all of you."

"You better hope we're not exposed, Janice," Dr. Sphinx replied. "Because we both know what will happen to you, to all of you, if the unaltered humans discover you exist. You think your cushy rooms with all the amenities are a harsh price? How about being strapped to a gurney, your torso splayed open so they can see what you look like on the inside?"

Emma put a hand to her mouth to stifle her gasp but couldn't stop the slight panic at the suggestion. As frightening as it was, there was an even worse nightmare. She knew what happened to freaks. They got put into cages and treated no better than animals. Prisoners to be used and abused.

She didn't want to be hurt ever again.

"You're assuming the humans will catch us," Barry retorted.

"And that they'll want to dissect us or put us in

cages," Janice added. "Could be they'll feel sorry for us and, instead, punish you."

"Considering the government has funded part of our research, they are more likely to kill you and bury you deep."

"Says you. I'll take that chance. Let me loose." Jacob was the one to reply.

"You know I can't. You all signed an agreement."

That contract and the moment flashed in her mind. She'd just left the hospital again, the prognosis not looking good, when that lawyer Lowry arrived with his briefcase. She'd barely read the fine print, just accepted the crib notes that said, in exchange for life-saving treatment, she'd remain with the Chimaeram Clinic for as long as the doctors in charge deemed necessary.

She was pretty good with forever, but not everyone liked that clause. They couldn't see the benefit in getting a free room, food, clothes, and entertainment. Apparently, some would prefer to return to the big bad world where everyone was selfish and hurtful.

Not Emma. She missed her safe room already. Violence brewed in the air. She could feel it in every breath she took, the familiarity not bringing any comfort, more a weary resignation. *Here we go again.*

Unless she could somehow fend off the impending chaos. "Will the new place be similar to the old one?" Emma asked.

"In some respects, yes. I'll make sure you'll have your own room again, Emma." She noticed how Sphinx's tone softened each time he spoke to her.

Yet for all his friendliness, he has never asked me to call him by his first name.

"Is that what it takes to get preferential treatment? Getting on our knees to suck your dick?" spat Janice.

The insult slapped. "I would never...He never..." gasped Emma, her cheeks heating. "He's like a father to me."

"Which makes it even sicker," muttered the man beside her.

"Dr. Sphinx is a kind and generous man," Emma hotly declared, only to be met with derisive laughter.

"Thank you, Emma, but not everyone is a model patient like you. Hence their poor opinion. And why this is necessary." The doctor approached Barry, needle upheld.

Barry strained again. "Like fuck are you doping my ass."

"You don't have a choice." Dr. Sphinx jabbed Barry and depressed the plunger. It took less than ten seconds of screamed invectives before the drug took effect and Barry slumped over.

"Who's next?" Dr. Sphinx grabbed another syringe from the wide-eyed nurse.

Janice gave him a baleful glare. "Is drugging women the only way you get laid?"

"You would know," Sphinx whispered loud enough to be heard as he tranqed her next.

Emma frowned. "What does he mean?"

It was Jacob who clued her in. "It means that the

man you consider a father takes his enjoyment with unconscious patients."

"But..." She blinked, doing her best to not relive the past. "But that's wrong." She looked at the doctor. "Tell them you would never do that." Except looking at his face, she realized it was the truth.

Sphinx lied to her face. "Don't listen to him. He's just making that up."

Only he wasn't. It was true, and with the knowledge, Emma's mind spun.

"Did you..." She couldn't ask. Couldn't bear to know.

As she looked into his face, at the satisfied smirk, a horrible sick feeling filled her. Her stomach tightened into a knot as her faith and trust suddenly shattered.

He hurt me.

He would hurt her again if he got the chance.

The very thought quickened her breath, and she fought against the multiplying dark spots dancing in front of her eyes.

Not again.

She took deep measured breaths that turned into pants as the doctor made the circuit, jabbing away with his needles, quieting all those who dared protest until he reached Emma.

He stared down at her, and she had to know for sure. Had to ask. "Did you do things to me while I slept?"

A bead of sweat rolled down the side of his face as

he opened his mouth. Even before he finished saying no, she blacked out.

When she came to, wind whistled through an open door. The guards were gone. Her shoulder hurt, and Sphinx lay dead on the floor. No point in checking for a pulse given his eyes stared sightlessly and his mouth remained pulled in a wide screaming rictus. Blood pooled around him.

A bad man now dead and good riddance. She didn't feel sorry for him at all. More ashamed she'd been fooled again.

Shudder. The helicopter trembled, and she glanced at the cockpit. Gaped to see the pilot slumped and the helicopter wobbling, as no one controlled it.

And I don't know how to fly.

She could only stare through the window as the ground rushed up to greet the chopper.

Then cry out as they hit the ground hard and darkness descended again.

CHAPTER ONE

THE FOLLOWING SPRING...

"I'll call you from the beach." Oliver lied about where he was going. Work, family, friends. They all thought he was taking an overdue vacation. Good thing none of them checked his luggage and saw the much warmer attire he'd stashed inside. He had a more interesting location to visit.

Ever heard of the Chimaeram Clinic? No? Neither had anyone else in the world. Yet, according to his source, a state-of-the-art medical facility had recently existed in the Rocky Mountains. It provided unsanctioned, highly illegal medical treatments to hundreds of people. Until it blew up.

Literally. Kaboom with plastic explosives.

There probably wasn't much of the clinic left. Especially given the harsh winter that just passed with record snowfalls. Didn't matter. Oliver still wanted to see it, but he had to do so in secret.

People had gone to great lengths to hide Chimaeram's existence, which meant there was an element of danger in exposing it.

Oliver didn't care. It wouldn't be the first time he'd gone deep undercover to lay bare a scandal. With the bounty on his head, he still didn't dare go anywhere near the Middle East, but he'd hung up his political cap a few years ago. Thought he'd never find something truly worthwhile to write about again. Until this story fell into his lap.

Illegal human experimentation. Something out of a science fiction movie and still happening to this day. The story would be huge, a bestseller for sure just like his previous novels.

If he could find some evidence.

The clinic itself didn't appear in any databases. No permits were ever issued for its construction. The land it sat on was technically owned by the crown.

If Oliver had not known its exact location—given by a source who was more than happy to spill everything he knew after imbibing a smuggled bottle of Scotch—he might have never found it. The most shocking part was the proximity to civilization.

For years, a mad scientist had experimented on people less than fifty miles into the Rocky Mountain range. And not just one doctor played God in that place. Although it was one doctor who started the travesty. Adrian Chimera–currently missing, hopefully dead, his Frankenstein secrets with him.

Despite his twisted medical vision, he'd had an

army of employees all culpable in his vile act. Some of those on his staff even shared in the treatment like Doctor Cerberus, who'd gone public with what they'd done. Oliver still remembered watching in jaw-dropped shock as the handsome man with the dark skin and youthful appearance spoke at length about the things he'd accomplished.

"I'm here today to tell you that science has found a cure. A cure for missing limbs. Comas. Even those lacking mental clarity."

"What kind of cure? Does it have any side effects?" a reporter had asked, her mien serious rather than incredulous at the boasting of an unknown doctor.

Cerberus had smiled. "The cure is multi-faceted and customized to the patient. As to side effects. Only minor things."

"You call that shit minor," exclaimed another reporter, pointing at the doctor.

The media event and the speech might have gone better if not for the pair of horns jutting from Cerberus's forehead and the glowing of his eyes.

Dr. Cerberus only ever presented the one speech. Then he disappeared from public sight. The media went nuts trying to locate him. Theories abounded, from his claim being the greatest prank of all time to more nefarious musings about government agencies nabbing him and either a) testing and questioning him under strict guard or b) autopsying his ass.

Unlike some, Oliver knew the truth. Cerberus was in hiding. Not with the government. It was worse than that. He'd joined up with a pharmaceutical company very interested in what he had to say and how they could use that information to make money, a concept Oliver couldn't comprehend.

The man was a monster, not just genetically but emotionally, too. Only someone truly depraved would have acted as Cerberus did. Taking innocent people—including his own daughter—some without the ability to speak for themselves, and conducting medical tests that were inhumane. Changing people into something else. Something *inhuman*.

He made monsters. Oliver knew this for a fact because the stupid bastards hired him to document their success. Gave him all the rope he needed to hang them.

A few of those poor patients had been recovered by the pharma company at great expense—mostly because greasing palms for silence was costly.

Those they brought back were caricatures of humanity—with a thirst for blood. Many weren't even recognizable as people. As part of his undercover investigation, Oliver had seen them—the woman with the beak who cawed and laid an egg every time she squatted. He tried to talk to them—the one called Fez, clacking the mandibles by the corners of his lips. Each time he left their presence horrified. An expression he hid lest those running the mad house restrict his access.

The joke was on them. The book he would write would bring about their doom. He had to destroy them before they took over where the Chimaeram Clinic had left off.

How does someone do that to a person? What kind of evil did it take to think it was okay to experiment on people?

According to Cerberus, it started because of one man. One literally sick man. Adrian Chimera, once a cripple with a debilitating disease, had cured himself with unproven medical science. Then went on a power-mad trip supposedly saving others.

But Chimera was out of business now. On the run. Possibly dead depending on the rumor you listened to. His staff, those that remained, had scattered. Their names and locations unknown. The lab he'd once lorded over as king, destroyed. The Chimera Secrets that survived gone into hiding.

That should have been the end of it. But evil ever did flourish when there was money to be made. And who better to take up the torch than a pharmaceutical company that needed something big to earn a huge payout?

Someone had to stop this harmful cure from spreading. Had to tell the world the truth. Which why, when the company hired Oliver to make a documentary and put a positive spin on things, he'd begun gathering evidence. Pictures. Reports. Interviews. Stuff acquired via less than honest methods.

His initial plan to expose the lies was ruined when all the info he'd been gathering disappeared. The files on his computer wiped clean as if they never existed.

The company owner, the same one who hired him, had given him a dressing down and reminded him to toe the line or pay the price.

He agreed.

In other words, he lied. *They think they can stop me.* On the contrary, they made him more determined to dig deeper. To go back to the place where it all began. Surely, he'd find evidence there.

The defunct Chimaeram Clinic wasn't easy to reach. Oliver didn't dare hire a helicopter, because someone would surely notice and either stop him, or follow. So how to reach the remote location? He did it the hard way: Driving as far as he could with an ATV. He'd had to ditch it far too soon when the going got steep. From that point on, he hiked with a heavy backpack. Hiked for two days.

Fifty some miles might not seem very far, as the crow flew, but on the ground, a ground that proved mountainous, each mile west involved going up through mountain passes before making progress. However, the grueling trek provided a reward when he crested that last pass and beheld the description that spilled from Cerberus's lips after a few glasses of Scotch.

"You'll know it when you see it. It's like a Garden of Eden. Lush and green. Seemingly untouched. The trees, towering monoliths opening onto a valley that is covered in grass. A weird thing to see in the mountains, and yet it's like a carpet. If you get there at the right time in spring, it blooms all over with tiny blue flowers."

"How did Chimera find it?" Oliver asked.

Cerberus shrugged. "Chance. Or maybe God did speak to him, after all. The things he could do, no man had ever thought of before."

God? Oliver almost scoffed but instead went after more info. "Describe more of this valley."

"It's beautiful." Such a strange thing to hear coming from the man who many in the media dubbed Satan. "There's a lake on the edge of it, with crystal-clear waters. But don't let it fool you. There're things swimming in there that will drag a man down."

"You going to claim he made mermaids, too?" Oliver scoffed, wondering how much he should believe.

"We only ever made one of those, and she left when the clinic blew up. I'm talking about other things. Dangerous things. Release the kraken!" Cerberus slapped the table, the harsh sound of it jarring.

And his exclamation surely a jest.

Scanning the valley at hand, Oliver noted a body of water free of waves, the surface crystal clear. As to being dangerous? He shook his head as he spotted a bird sitting on its surface. More likely there was some invisible undertow that proved deadly. The only fish that usually attacked humans were sharks and most didn't live in icy waters. He didn't have to dip a toe to know the water would be frigid. Lakes that formed in the mountain from run-offs never went much above freezing, meaning hypothermia was a very real danger even if the submersion lasted only a few minutes.

Heading down the side of the mountain he was

quickly enveloped by a forest. He paid attention as he travelled through the thick woods, what was left of them. The once tall forest had suffered a tragedy. The burnt stumps attested to the raging fire that had whipped through and left devastation in its wake. It must have occurred before the winter, as the ashy remains had turned to a sodden muck and already tough green shoots sought to reclaim the land.

The wide burn swath led him right to the grassy field where the remnants of an oval track remained visible, the area not yet recovered from the many feet that once used to wear it down to bare dirt.

Conscious the sun was getting low in the sky, Oliver quickened his pace, aiming past the track and the strip of grass for the concrete pad, barren of vehicles, and a stark stain worse than the fire because it was manmade.

The true object of his quest? The pile of rubble where a building once stood. Nature already sought to reclaim it, hints of green staining the stone. Leaves were caught in the crevices, and a hint of despair hovered over it all.

He couldn't help but head straight for it, placing his hand on the broken frame of what might have been a window. Excited and, at the same time, shocked because as he'd trekked these past few days, he'd wondered just how much of what Cerberus said was the truth.

Because everyone knows the devil lies.

Despite his excitement, Oliver set up his camp

first, pitching a tent on the concrete, using his light yet sturdy hammer to bang in the spikes, not caring of the cracks it created. His temporary home ready, he then unpacked his bag of all the necessities. Not just the rations and spare warm clothes he'd brought. He'd used up valuable space and weight in order to bring his laptop, a camera, and even his phone.

Given what happened to the last batch of information he'd gathered, this time he didn't plan to wait to spread the information. He'd brought along a satellite phone, which meant a signal—a weak one—even this far from civilization. He'd be live streaming his findings. Tweeting out images. Showing the world the secrets that someone was determined to bury.

With the internet as his witness, this time there would be no hiding it. Once it hit the web, the evidence would live forever!

Phone in hand, Oliver backtracked across the field and began his live stream. "Hey, everybody." A simple address given his channel currently had no followers. "I'm here in the valley of monsters." A name he'd coined, which he hoped would draw attention. "The place where Adrian Chimera and his compatriot, Aloysius Cerberus, used to have their lab." He didn't call them doctors. It seemed wrong to give them that kind of lofty title. "As you can see, they chose a gorgeous but very out-of-the-way place to conduct their work." He walked through the devastated forest, making sure he panned wide to give the audience a good view.

"You can't reach this place by road. It's helicopter

or hiking only. And not an easy hike, I should add. You have to go through dangerous terrain. Which made it easier to hide what they were doing for so long." He pivoted to show the mountains behind him and the devastation.

"You can see some kind of fire ripped through here. Intentional? Possibly. Especially given what happened to the clinic itself." Pivoting again, he made sure to focus on the rubble of the building, the heap unmistakably manmade. "They tried to destroy the evidence of what they did. But I'm here to expose the truth. To show you why we must prevent this from happening again. Why we must stop the monsters that already roam among us. The fate of the world depends on it."

Ending the live stream, Oliver tucked the phone in his pocket and eyeballed the ruins. He wondered if it would be stable enough for him to enter. He'd brought only limited spelunking equipment. Hopefully enough for him to descend into the remains of the clinic and get some truly epic photos. A body or two would truly be a coup. Especially if they were only partially human.

Speaking of pics... He glanced at the sky and the sun almost fully set, the last of its rays, streaks of pink and orange along the far horizon. The perfect time of day to get some truly magnificent and artistic shots. After all, every scandal needed beauty to bring out the starkness of the ugly acts.

Oliver whipped out his camera—a must-have despite the premium space it took in his pack—and fiddled a moment with the lens before he began snapping a multitude of shots.

Click. Click. He whirled side to side, aiming up, down, trying to get as many angles as possible. The sun sank past the ridgeline, and darkness descended, but that was fine. He had more than enough battery left in his laptop—thanks to the solar charger.

He tossed the camera in his tent and spent the next hour eating and typing some notes. Not much yet to talk about. People wouldn't be interested in the uninteresting hike. The truly meaty part of his quest would happen tomorrow. Still, he documented the journey, because while his main goal might be exposing the truth—and putting a stop to it—the book itself needed some kind of build-up to the main event.

Yawning, his body tired after several hard days of exertion, Oliver crawled into his tent, his sleeping bag providing welcome warmth given how sharply the temperature still dropped at night. Of course, having decided to go to bed, he couldn't sleep. Hence why he reached over, grabbed his camera, and transferred the images to his laptop. He began going through the shots, discarding the shit ones, storing the maybes in a folder.

He saw it just before the end. A strangeness that had him pinching his screen to zoom. The enlarged image made even less sense.

Oliver saw a girl.

Or so it seemed. Her features were delicate, eyes huge. She appeared to be peering at him from behind the hump of the destroyed clinic, her face barely visible in the growing shadows.

He swiped to the next picture. Too blurry. The next, there she was again with her big elfin eyes, the glow of them almost purple.

And projecting from her forehead...a fucking horn.

CHAPTER TWO

Emma ducked out of sight before the male could see her. At least she stood downwind, far enough away he couldn't scent her. But she could smell him. It was what drew her from her hiding place. A scent that didn't belong and roused her curiosity—along with fear.

He was the first non-patient she'd seen since the crash, and he came armed—with a camera!

He took pictures of the rubble. She understood the act, just like she grasped it was a bad thing. Unlike some of the others who'd crashed with her, Emma's mind remained sharp. When they'd recovered from the wrecked helicopter—most of them at any rate—they ran off together. Safety in numbers, unless those you travelled with got hungry. She still remembered when Janice snapped. Barry never stood a chance and almost didn't recover.

But Janice wasn't alone in reverting to a more

primal state. Some of the others on the chopper had allowed themselves to devolve in their quest for survival.

Not Emma. She kept herself alert and wouldn't give in to the darkness lurking within, which was why she recognized the danger the man posed.

Rather than confront him, she escaped into the rubble of the clinic, not needing any light to guide her steps. She knew every broken inch intimately. This had been her home since she'd stumbled back to it at the start of winter. This would be her home forever.

If she could get rid of the intruder. Before she made it to her hidey-hole, she stopped. Chewed her lower lip as logic hammered at her fear.

Running away wouldn't solve her problem. What if he'd seen her? Or took more pictures, of things no one should see? Then more people would come. With guns. And cages. They would want to examine her. There would be pain involved. Tears. Blood—lots of blood and scrubbing involved.

I have to go back.

The very idea made her heart stutter, and her mouth dried to the point her tongue got stuck. The spots she dreaded danced before her eyes. She shook her head to dispel them lest they consume her.

I will not let panic win. A mantra she repeated over and over until calmness settled over her again. With that serenity came the ability to creep back through the ruins of her home until she reached the top level, the one just below the worst of the rubble.

Pausing, she listened. Listened for a good long while. When living in the wild, those who lived longest didn't rush in.

Emma took her time, listening to the soughing of wind through the cracks of debris. The chirps of bugs just emerging to embrace a crisp spring night. When a long moment passed without a sound, she crept higher, pausing to peek from the rubble. Rather than the usual darkness coating the valley, she saw a few spots of light by the old helicopter pad.

He'd made a camp, which implied he came prepared. Possibly planned to stick around for a while. Unless she made things unpleasant for him.

Slowly. Quietly. Carefully. She crept closer.

Closer.

The dying embers of his fire drew her like a moth to the flame, the heat welcome. She hadn't dared light too many of them in the ruins, not just because of the carbon dioxide and smoke. There were things that lived in there with Emma. Things best left alone.

The intruder had not left anything outside. Not even his pack. Especially not his camera. She eyed the tent he'd erected, the flap zipped closed, and yet she could see a hint of light coming from the seams, a subtle glow through fabric.

What crap luck. He had all his electronics in there with him.

She edged nearer, her skin prickling, letting her know she wasn't the only pair of eyes watching. For the most part, the predators in this place left her alone. After all, in many respects, she was just like them.

In others, she wasn't. For one, she didn't have the urge to kill and chew on raw flesh. Not long after the cure began to work, she'd made the choice to become a vegetarian, which made the passing winter hard. Good thing she'd managed to scavenge some leftover supplies in the clinic. Despite the utter destruction above, there was much below ground that the explosion hadn't touched. It meant she found canned foods, bottled beverages, even a massive bag of rice that slowly dwindled.

With summer coming, she'd soon be able to forage for fresher items. Never mind she had no idea what she'd find to eat. It wasn't as if there were orchards or gardens around. But that kind of thinking led to panic, which led to...yeah. Best not dwell on that right now.

Only paces from the tent, she froze as she heard a rustle from within. She heard the *zzzz* of the zipper being lowered a second before she moved. Emma ducked behind the tent, her heart pounding so loud he'd surely hear.

He stumbled from the tent, grumbling something about, "Shouldn't have drank the last of my canteen."

He went off a way, staggering right to the edge of the helicopter pad before stopping to relieve himself. Knowing she had limited time, Emma popped her head into his tent, saw the camera sitting inside, and snatched it. She'd just managed to hide herself behind his tent again, clutching the camera, doing her best not to hyperventilate, when he stumbled back to his bed.

Zzzzz. The zipper shut him in, and she almost sighed in relief. Best not get complacent too quickly. She wasn't safe yet.

Camera tucked close, she almost ran back to the rubble. However, haste led to mistakes. She needed to always be aware lest she be caught by surprise. While nothing confronted her, noises taunted her, eyes watched, and she didn't feel safe again until she was in her hidey-hole.

Only then did she raise the camera, ready to smash it to pieces, destroying whatever images it held. She paused with her hand raised.

Moments later, she scrolled through pictures. Scenery for the most part but occasional selfie shots of a man. A handsome man with the beginnings of a beard and an earnest face.

Seeing him—another living, breathing person— brought a pang. How long since she'd talked to someone?

Months.

Even longer since she'd been involved romanti- cally, mostly because she had problems getting close to men. Her broken childhood made it hard to trust. Was it any wonder that she grabbed tight to the first guy who showed her kindness? Only it turned out to be a sham. The first time he tried to pimp her out, she ran. But it happened again. Not always with the pimping but the wrong choices. The wrong men who seemed to think it was okay to hit when they were frustrated. Who thought a girlfriend shouldn't have the word "no" in her vocabulary. By her late twenties, she gave up.

No more relationships. Rather than looking for love, she started to love herself. Put herself and her needs first. Cleaned up her act. Her life started to get better, so wouldn't you know, she got sick. Really sick to the point she was told she would die.

The irony almost made her walk into traffic. Why fight anymore? Some people obviously weren't destined for a happy life.

She had just about given up when a miracle happened. Someone offered her a second chance, and it wouldn't cost her a penny. She didn't have to spread her legs. She, Emma Kylie Baker, was offered an opportunity to live. She didn't blink or balk at the rules and contracts surrounding it.

For the first time in her life, she won. But she didn't let herself fall back into her old patterns. Even once Dr. Chimera cured her, she chose to stick to her vow and not get involved. Not for lack of opportunity. The guards at the clinic did occasionally flirt. One of the female nurses did, too. But Emma never let it go any further. Didn't want to. She'd been happy to live in her little bubble. Warm and fed, stress free for once in her life.

Her life now was kind of similar in that respect. Quiet. With no one to harass her or make demands.

It should have been paradise, yet, of late, she'd been

feeling blue. Seeing the man tonight, it finally hit her why.

She, who hated socializing and had issues with trust, missed people. Found herself craving real conversation. Longing for the human contact of another.

In her clinic days, the doctors who came to check on her progress always spent a moment chatting. The nurses who took her vitals provided idle chatter and gossip. The television, while it was one-sided, also provided contact with people.

Now? All Emma had was the wind in the trees and the eyes that watched her. Eyes belonging to bodies that had long since lost their ability to discourse in anything other than grunts and howls. A few couldn't even manage that anymore.

Sometimes she wondered what set her apart from them.

Sometimes she wished she could be just as mindless.

Instead, she was alone and finally tired of the solitude, which might be why she fell asleep with her hand resting on the face of the man smiling into the screen of the camera.

CHAPTER THREE

THE SUNSHINE LIGHTING THE INSIDE OF HIS TENT woke him early the next morning. After taking care of business, Oliver started a fire and, while it got going, rummaged in his tent for his camera.

"Where the fuck is it? I know I put it right there," Oliver exclaimed aloud, glaring at the empty corner. Except now it was missing. Nothing else had vanished, though.

"She took it!" There was no doubt in his mind that the strange woman he'd seen in the images he'd taken must have stolen it. The question was, did she steal it purposely, knowing what it could do? Or was it more of a magpie impulse?

Having studied many of the Chimera projects picked up and placed under observation, he knew most of them were driven by primal impulse. Interview attempts failed because they lacked basic communication skills and possessed only rudimentary cognition.

The true measure of how far they'd fallen showed in their less-than-stellar hygiene. Even when given the opportunity to bathe, most chose to remain in their own filth.

Because monsters don't take baths. Not an insult but the simple truth. The exception being Cerberus. He was probably the only known example of a Chimera project who took care of himself. And Oliver had to wonder how long it would last.

He remembered their last interview. The doctor's behavior grew more and more erratic.

"Have you ever wondered why vampires drink blood straight from the vein?" Cerberus asked, rather than reply when asked what creature he'd mixed his DNA with.

"No."

"People have argued that they do it because they must feed from only the fresh stuff. Which is nonsense. The same nutrients exist whether it's sucked from a donor or a bag."

Realizing Cerberus wouldn't get back on track until they followed the train of thought, Oliver said, "So why do most legends have them drinking from the neck?"

"Because it's fun," said Cerberus, his lips stretching in a wide grin, the canines on each side definitely more pronounced than normal.

The more sanity slipped from Cerberus, the more his differences became pronounced. His horns grew, as did a tail, and recently they'd seen a hump across his shoulder blades that they predicted would turn into wings.

Which led Oliver to wonder, did the lack of mental acuity bring out the monster? Or was it the other way around?

Not that it mattered. Once he showed the world that the Chimera Secrets—as he'd dubbed them and which would probably be the title of his book—were a sham, they would put an end to this sick science. An end to the pharmaceutical company that sought to exploit the perverse.

"All right, horn girl, you might have stolen my camera, but I still have my phone," Oliver muttered as he plugged it into the solar charger and exited the tent to place it in the sun. His laptop joined it. While they gobbled up the sun's rays and turned them into energy, he prepped breakfast. The ring of stones he set the night before provided a containment area for the load of branches and dry grass he dumped on the hungry flames. Smoke billowed for a moment, before the fire truly got going. He grabbed his pot—and a gun—before he headed for the lake.

With his fatigue the night before, he'd avoided the large body of water. Despite his disbelief and mockery of Cerberus's silly warning, he did remain wary of it and had no plans to go for a swim.

The morning air proved crisp and fresh, only the faint whiff of smoke from his fire marring it. No sound other than the occasional insect. Nor had he spotted anything living since the bird he'd seen sitting atop the water when he arrived the day before, which seemed odd in a valley this verdant. Could be the fire had spooked them out of the area. After all, burned foliage didn't provide much forage, but that was only true for part of the valley. Could it be the faint whiff of smoke kept them from coming near?

Or they know something I don't.

As for the face in the pictures? Probably a trick of a tired mind and shadows. Chances were a second look at them in the light of day would have shown him imagining things.

Nobody lived here.

Kneeling on the shore of the lake, Oliver admired the clarity of the water as he dipped his hand in it. No surprise it was shockingly cold, reinforcing his theory that it was fed from melting snow of the icy caps crowning the mountains. He wondered how deep it went. He could see the pebbled bottom here at the edge, but farther out, it got murky. Usually a sign of great depth.

He filled his pot but, before heading back to his camp, took a moment to scoop some water and wash his face. It chilled the skin but refreshed at the same time. It had been days since he'd properly bathed, which was why he set his pot on the fire to boil and returned to the lake's edge with a cloth and a bio-friendly bar of soap. Laying his gun down first, he stripped to his boxers, conscious of the fact someone —*she*—might be watching. At least he had nothing to be ashamed of. He kept himself fit despite his age, nearing forty. And his recent months of working inside hadn't managed to make him soft.

Oliver crouched down and doused his cloth before rubbing it with soap. He scrubbed himself. Chest. Arms. Even thrust that wet rag down his boxers for a quick clean that made him shrivel. Then he did it again with a rinsed cloth, wiping the soapy remains.

Feeling clean, if chilled, he hurriedly sluiced the cloth again, so it would be clean for drying. He swirled it through water, causing ripples, which might be why he never saw it coming.

The tentacle lashed out of the water and narrowly missed him.

"Jesus fucking Christ!" He landed on his ass on the pebbled beach, staring in disbelief at the waving appendage. Much like an octopus, it had mottled pinkish skin and suckers on the underside. Problem was it appeared way larger than an octopus arm had the right to be, not to mention it was hundreds of miles from the nearest ocean.

Expecting it to sink back into the water, he was stunned when it hovered in midair as if sniffing before it jabbed in his direction. He managed to roll out of its way, fingers scrabbling and missing the gun hidden under his clothes. He yelled as another appendage shot out of the lake and wrapped its slimy tip around his leg.

It immediately dragged him toward the water, despite the fingers he dug into the ground trying to halt his progress. With his free foot, he kicked at the tentacle. But while the one holding him loosened, the second one slapped at him, the suckers suctioning to skin, startling a pained cry from him.

"Shoo!" a feminine voice yelled. Not that the lake monster paid her any mind. It did, however, take issue with the rocks tossed at it. Huge hunks of concrete went flying overhead, some to hit the gelatinous arms, others to land precariously close to Oliver's head. But it helped.

The tentacles sank back into the watery depths, and he spent a moment staring at the once again still surface.

"What the fuck was that?"

He kind of expected the woman to reply. After all, she'd saved his life. Only there was no answer, and when he hopped to his feet, moving away from the dangerous lake, he didn't spot anyone at all.

She'd fled.

"Where did you go?" Yeah, he was talking aloud to himself again. A man who'd been alone in the world for a few days needed someone to chat with. He'd learned that truth a while ago when he'd gotten caught in a war-torn country and had to hide out in a cave for almost three months.

Between the lake and his campsite, there weren't many places to hide. He took his time and checked them, including his tent, in case she'd chosen to surprise him.

But his tent was empty of bodies, and as for the devices he had sitting in the sun? His phone was gone, along with his laptop.

"Fucking freaking..." He ran out of words at that point. What to call her? He couldn't resort to something nasty because she'd damned well saved his life. He had no doubt that thing would have dragged him in and drowned him.

He wasn't even sure if it was the same woman he'd seen with that thing sticking out of her head. However, now she'd ensured he'd track her down. Stealing his shit.

"Not cool, lady," he shouted out, in case she watched. "Stealing isn't nice."

Neither was the fact he'd see her put in a cage or put down just for existing. For a moment shame gripped him, but he hardened himself against it. *Nothing personal, but humanity can't afford to let monsters roam free.*

Speaking of monsters, what the fuck was in that lake? Cerberus had once yelled something about a kraken, but he'd not taken him seriously. Only thing he was sure of? It definitely was not a mermaid.

Was the thing that attacked him a Chimera secret project, too? Or just a coincidence? After all, Canada had its version of the Loch Ness monster known as the Ogopogo. Wouldn't it be ironic if he'd actually found a legend?

Whatever it was, it would make fetching water dangerous, and forget any full-body baths. At least forewarned meant being better prepared next time.

Oliver grabbed the machete slash axe he used to do a variety of shit—hack branches for firewood, whack long grass, defend against rabid ninja squirrels--and returned to the lake's edge to snatch his clothes. The water remained still, and as if to mock him, the damned bird was back, floating atop the surface, not a care in the world.

"Tease," he muttered before heading back to his campsite and the now madly boiling pot of water. Digging in a tin, he pulled out a sealed baggie with his dwindling supply of coffee. Maybe a few more days left before he ran out. Which was fine. He only needed a few days to crack open this secret, find his fucking phone, and call for a ride. Because by then it wouldn't matter who knew about the clinic. The more people who came looking for it, the better.

The acrid coffee went down like a burning trail of lava, but he didn't dare sputter. He might have an audience. So he smacked his lips and made a show of enjoying it. If the woman had been living out here since the clinic blew up last fall, then how had she survived? What did she eat? Drink? She obviously knew of the danger in the lake. He'd be sure to ask when he hunted her down.

Setting the cup aside, he tore open the top of his breakfast pack. He poured some hot water into his dehydrated MRI. It went from strange, lumpy, colored bits to fluffy and moist, the fake smell of bacon wafting. Some kind of scrambled mash that resembled dog vomit. Tasted okay, though. Anyone who claimed to enjoy those foil-sealed meals lied. It was barely palatable, but when he couldn't hunt or forage, it provided all the nutrients he needed and kept his belly from rebelling hungrily. It also weighed almost nothing and barely took up any room.

Given the MRIs were in limited supply, he couldn't waste them. He had been supplementing his meals with the wildlife he caught—rabbit and a fish thus far. The dandelions the day before had made a decent salad once he dumped vinegar and salt on it.

Despite his urgency when it came to regaining his electronics, he spent a moment setting up a few snares. Hopefully he'd catch something that he could roast before night. He wasn't looking forward to his choice between goulash and some kind of beef stew.

What the woman didn't know was his waterproof watch was connected to his phone. So long as she didn't destroy it, then he might be able to track it down.

He had a feeling she'd gone into the ruins, so he fully equipped himself, ensuring the pockets of his vest were filled with useful stuff. Compass. Lighter. Even a few glow sticks. He put on his tool belt replete with carabiner, a loop of rope, and a sheath with his smaller knife. He also made sure to strap on his holster, the magazine in the gun fully loaded. He wouldn't be caught unaware again.

Heading to the mound of rubble, he glanced over at the forest, the only other place she could have fled, but that would have required a lot of speed to make it before he'd turned around. It seemed unlikely. Then again, that mega lake monster should have been impossible, too.

He cast a glance to the other side of the valley where the forest hadn't been touched by fire. It loomed thick and ominous, the old kind of forest seen in fairy tales that hid all manner of magical creatures.

Monsters that the knights were sent in to slay.

I am the knight. Now he just needed to find the beast in the ruins. Yes, beast, because he couldn't let her feminine appearance fool him. He wouldn't be distracted or seduced.

Who is she? How long had she been using the clinic as a shelter? Was she alone?

After the harsh winter they'd just gone through, it was doubtful many of Chimera's secrets had survived. He'd certainly not witnessed many signs of life. Not the large kind at any rate. Only the smaller animals you'd expect to see: squirrels, rabbits, birds. Which, in retrospect, was kind of odd. He'd not once seen any droppings of bear or deer, which he would have assumed to be plentiful in this area.

In his early twenties, he'd done a stint as a forest ranger—cracking a poaching ring—in a similar type of terrain in Colorado. His rebellion years, his mother called it. In a sense, that was accurate. He'd wanted to get away from his family and the noise of the cities.

In the woods, there was no one to care if he grew out his beard or wore the same shirt two days in a row. Just man against nature. So why hadn't he stayed in the woods?

Family. They had an evil way of sucking you back in.

The bright morning light put the ruins in stark relief. Oliver spent a moment studying the remains of the once two-story clinic. Shards of glass, those not yet buried by weather and vegetation, glinted in the sun like shattered jewels littering the ground. Throughout the broken chunks of concrete he could see the tendrils of wiring, the rusted remains of metal rebar, the inner guts you'd see of any building, including the projecting tip of a coat rack.

According to Cerberus's testimony, the top floors belonged to management. No surprise there. The big, shiny offices went to the evil doctors. It was below ground, out of sight of electronic eyes in the sky, that the true science happened. Employee and supply levels first then several laboratory and patient ones. So much evidence waiting for him to find if any of it survived the blast.

Fucking Chimera. Knowing he was about to be exposed, he had done his best to destroy the clinic.

According to Cerberus, Chimera—paranoid that he'd one day be discovered—had implemented a self-destruct option, seeding his clinic with explosive charges. What Cerberus didn't know was if all those bombs had gone off. *"He installed those close to a decade ago and, as far as I know, never upgraded them again. Could be they didn't all explode. Or maybe he only demolished the top portion and the basement remained intact."*

"How do you even know all this? I thought you were gone by the time he evacuated."

Cerberus smiled. "I have my sources."

What Cerberus never revealed was why he turned on his partner. Almost two decades they'd worked together, and yet something changed. Enough that Cerberus decided to risk it all and go public.

A good thing or the world might have never known the monsters were living among them.

"Let's see if Chimera's plan failed." Could Oliver gain entry underground?

The ruin itself appeared to have points of access. The trampled grass and spots worn clean gave the access points away. Someone obviously travelled in and out. He was going to wager that there were cave-like pockets inside. A hidey-hole for the woman.

Could also be something else. Hell, there could be a whole bunch of mutants hiding in the ruins. The grim reminder had him checking his holster. The feel of his gun reassured. If he ran into something dangerous, he'd handle it. Not much could rise from a bullet to the head.

Wishing he had his phone to do a video, Oliver made a circuit of the rubble, paying close attention to the areas that seemed to have the most traffic. Dropping to one knee, he eyed an impression left in the soft spongy ground, still wet from the spring melt, in the shape of a foot. A small foot. Just the right size to match that of a petite woman, he'd bet.

The footprint emerged from a spot where the concrete chunks leaned against one another, forming a triangle of shadow. He tapped the button on his headband, and the lamp at his forehead shone brightly.

He stepped into the rubble-strewn cave, only it was more like a maze than a cave he soon realized. There was a slit at the back, and he entered to find himself in a narrow passage. He made it a few paces before he came to a fork in the debris.

Follow the passage straight or take the hole to his left? He crouched and took a peek inside. It went a short way then appeared to open up somewhere bright with sunlight. It was the charging cord caught in a crack, one he'd wager had ripped free of his phone as someone passed through with it, that decided him.

He popped into a tiny pocket open to the sky with the remnants of drywall on the ground. Threading through it, he found cleared paths, going two ways into new tunnels. Left and right.

Which way to go?

He chose left mostly because he was left-handed. He ran into a dead end soon after, the fall of concrete appearing fresh, showing just how unstable this ruin was.

How stupid he probably was for wandering around in it, and to do what?

I am going to prove the existence of monsters. Make the world realize there is a serious crisis at hand.

I could have done that back home.

Maybe. He'd lost his access to the monster files and Cerberus. However, just because his initial source of information had dried up didn't mean he couldn't have pursued other avenues of research. The problem was avoiding scrutiny. He was supposed to be writing a book. A book meant words saved in a file. A file they could probably access and read.

Hence why he pretended to go on vacation. Hopped a plane then switched at an airport. Then switched again. Hoping to lose anyone who might have followed and praying they wouldn't realize he'd used a fake ID. He picked up a new phone. New number. Created new social media accounts that wouldn't lead back to him. He was ready to create the next viral sensation.

But, for that, he had to find some evidence. Proof of the things he'd learned. The danger humans were in.

If only he could get his hands on a living specimen...

"Where are you hiding, Horn Girl?" he muttered aloud as he backtracked and took the other route. It quickly grew tricky to maneuver, the spots between the debris getting tighter, and yet he ignored the voice that urged caution and kept pressing forward. Going deeper until all the light was gone and only his head-lamp illuminated the way. But he knew he was on the right track. He found a strand of hair caught on a rough edge of rock.

He was looking ahead and stepping over a hump of broken ceiling tile and drywall when he almost fell in the hole. The middle of his foot hit the edge, and he teetered on the lip of a chasm. He swallowed hard as he stared down at the bottomless pit ready to swallow him whole.

I refuse to die because I fell in a pit. If he was going to end up a blurb in a paper, then it better be for something good.

Stepping back, he knelt down and shone the light below, the beam bouncing over more broken shit, illuminating the particles of dust that had yet to settle. But best of all, he saw a way down. There were no stairs or rope to rappel with, but the wreckage formed a convenient sloping pile that he gingerly stepped on, expecting at any moment it would shift and send him sliding.

He made it to the floor and had to tamp down his excitement as he realized he had found access to the first basement level. Not the most important one. This was where Cerberus claimed the employees congregated for meals, entertainment, and had their living quarters.

There were more signs of usage here, the area cleared, the sloping pile comprised of a variety of junk from chairs and tables and drywall to hunks of the floor that had fallen through.

But no sign of the woman or any kind of life yet. Shining his light around, he saw at least three points of exit.

Rather than play eenie, meenie, miny, moe, he went about it logically. Left opening first. Quickly ended, given it led to a mostly collapsed room full of electrical boxes, now dead. The next archway didn't fare much better, and while he could have shifted stuff to move farther inside, he doubted the woman had come through here recently. Which left one last door.

Upon entering, he noticed the difference. The hallway was clear of junk but, most fascinating of all, another hole in the floor. This one actually had a ladder of sorts created from wiring tied and braided together. It was tethered top and bottom, nice and taut, so it didn't wobble too much as he climbed down.

It showed thought, which was more than he'd ever seen from the monsters in that lab. Perhaps the woman hiding was more like Cerberus. Still cognitive, and yet losing her humanity daily.

Tracking her progression might make an even better story. But first he had to find her and his stuff!

It finally occurred to him to load the app on his watch called *Find your phone, dumbass*. It literally had him as an ass on the screen, a tiny bare one. The phone was a flashing beacon.

When it worked.

He frowned at his watch. It didn't show a single blinking thing. That didn't bode well. Either she'd destroyed it or the phone was hidden too deep for a signal to make its way out.

The level he'd just entered appeared oddly intact. A few ceiling tiles on the floor and furniture turned over, yet the massive room still stood. The light on his forehead danced around showing him the giant screens bolted to the wall, the couches. The trestle table and benches. Which meant beyond this room, according to

Cerberus, was the personal quarters for staff. Which put the elevator—he whirled—behind him. The doors were wedged open, providing an ominous portal to the lower levels.

But should he go there before he'd explored this one first?

It wouldn't hurt to do a quick search.

Especially since he was a little confused. The way Cerberus spoke, the first level underground should have been the habitat one. So which floor had he just left? Could it be there was a utility level between the main building and the basement itself? Could that level have been the buffer that protected what hid underneath?

It certainly seemed that way given how intact this section appeared to be. Still he treaded carefully from the middle of the room, glancing from time to time overhead, conscious of the precariously piled weight pushing down. He made it to the far side without getting crushed and found himself at an intersection. Straight ahead, a cave-in. But to his left and right, more hallways, each projecting an ominous aura with their dangling wires and dead lights.

Cerberus said the women were housed in the west wing. It seemed only logical he start there first. Most of the doors were open, and a glance inside showed rooms quickly emptied. Drawers left open, a few with scraps of fabric hanging out. The beds unmade. So many places for someone—or something—to hide.

After the third room, he realized it would take him

forever to search every single room, nook, and cranny. Yet what else could he do? He kept moving, his steps faster and faster as he weaved in and out, quickly getting a sense for the places to peek. All the rooms followed the same layout. There were too many of them. So many people working with those sick doctors.

And this was just the women's wing. How many more on the other side?

Turning at an intersection, he finally found some destruction. Farther down, the hallway had caved in, and the doorways closest to it were crushed. So of course, this was the place he heard a rustle.

The slightest of sound, yet the first sign of life he'd heard. Could be a simple shifting of debris. A rodent who'd made its home here. Or maybe his first break.

"Who's there? Show yourself!" he called out, despite the folly of advertising his location. He had his gun in hand, ready to fire. Straining, he sought to capture any sound at all.

As if to mock him, the silence thickened, pressing down on him, along with the tons of concrete over his head.

He stepped closer to one of the ruined doors. It had buckled so that there was a slit wide enough for a person to get through if they crouched. A great hiding spot.

Balancing on the balls of his feet, he lowered himself, the light on his head bobbing, stabbing into the dark hole, illuminating nothing but more darkness. He didn't discern any movement, nor the freaky glare of red rat eyes, yet the hairs on the back of his neck rose. Something watched him. While not prone to flights of fancy, he couldn't deny a sense of malevolence.

He crept closer to the doorway, doing his best to filter the shadows to see what lay beyond. He had no doubt he'd found something. Maybe even the woman.

A stench wafted from the opening. Moist and earthy, unlike the dry dust of the previous rooms he'd visited before.

"I don't want to hurt you." Could the thing hiding hear the lie?

There was a rustle and an exhalation as if a deep breath blown out, and fetid heat washed over him. Gross.

His grip tightened on the gun. Much as he wanted to document a monster, he wouldn't hesitate to kill if it presented a danger.

More rustling, and his finger tightened on the trigger. "I know you're here."

"Don't shoot!" The soft whisper from behind almost had the opposite effect.

He whirled and blinked as his light illuminated the woman in all her glory.

There she was. In the flesh. And projecting from her forehead a big honking horn. He'd found the unicorn lady.

CHAPTER FOUR

THE BRIGHT LIGHT BEAMING FROM THE MAN'S forehead blinded, and Emma blinked before shading her eyes with her hand. It blocked some of the glare but couldn't hide the thing sticking out of her forehead.

The guy stared. It took him a long moment before he said, "What are you?"

"Isn't the correct question, *who* am I?" The fact he didn't see her as a person shouldn't have surprised. Not many people did.

Even before she went to stay at the clinic, the world had turned a blind eye to the woman beaten down by life. A perpetual victim who wasn't worthy of their care.

At the clinic, she became a bit of a celebrity with the doctors and nurses but not because of who she was. They were fascinated by what she became.

"Who are you?" He slipped the headband down around his neck and then twisted it around to his back, giving her some respite. No longer a unicorn in a headlight.

"My name is Emma Kylie Baker."

"I'm Oliver."

An awkward silence stretched that they both interrupted with, "Why are you here?"

She giggled as they slammed the quiet with the same question. "I'm here because I have nowhere else to go."

"You were a patient of the Chimaeram Clinic?"

The knowledge of the clinic meant he wasn't a random hiker. She thought about denying it, but what was the point? She nodded, which only served to draw his attention to her abnormality. "The doctors brought me here to cure me."

"And instead made you into a monster." His lip curled.

A pang of sadness hit. To think she'd started to feel lonely enough that she'd approached him. His expression and attitude said it all. She could never live in society again. This lonely life was the best she could hope for.

Stop it with the pity party already. Don't let this jerk bring you down.

Her chin tilted. "I'd do it again. It was this"—she indicated her horn—"or dying. I think I got the better end of the deal."

Her words brought a frown to his face. "You were injured?"

She shrugged. "Of a sort." An unhealthy childhood

followed by a similar stint in her adult years, along with bad genes, made for the worst-case scenario. "Why are you here?"

"Because the world needs to know what happened in this place, so it never happens again," he declared, bringing to life her worst fear.

"You can't tell anyone."

Rather than reply to her statement, he asked, "Where's my stuff?"

"What stuff?" She tucked her hands behind her back, suddenly very aware of the phone she'd stuffed in her pocket. She only barely nabbed it, distracted by the image of him bathing—the lean muscular lines of his body drawing her eye. The fact she stared was the only reason she felt compelled to save him when the creature of the lake tried to eat him.

"I want my phone, laptop, and camera back. You had no right to steal them."

The accusation stung, yet what choice did he leave her? "You were taking pictures."

"And? It's not a crime."

No, however it could prove deadly to her if he made public the wrong kind of picture. Emma knew she remained safe only because people didn't know about her or the others hiding at the clinic and in the surrounding areas. If word got out...this place would be overrun, and then where would she go?

"If I give you back your stuff, will you leave?"

"No."

The truth took her aback. "You don't have permission to be here."

"Neither do you."

Her shoulders squared. "I live here."

"I wouldn't call this living."

Her annoyance with him made her regret saving him that morning. "I should have let the thing in the lake eat you."

"It was you that saved me?"

"Yes. Which means you owe me."

"I'm not letting you keep my stuff as thanks." He sounded quite firm on that point.

"How about just leaving me alone? Pretending we never met."

His lips flattened. "I can't do that."

"Why?"

He raked fingers through his hair. "It's complicated."

A non-answer to go along with his determination to expose her.

He's a threat. Which made it hard to understand why, when the darkness began oozing from the doorway, instead of letting it swallow him whole, she gave warning. "We need to get out of here." She'd been too intent on Oliver to notice any other danger.

He shook his head. "I'm not leaving until I get answers."

"No. I mean it. You have to leave right now. Before it gets you." She grabbed his arm and tugged, pulling him away from the shadow behind him that deepened, the edges creeping up the wall, flooding across the floor in a stain that would absorb anything organic in its path.

He ripped free of her grip with a frown. "What the hell, lady? You can't tell me what to do. I'm here to expose the monstrosities that happened here."

"Awesome. Great. Go ahead. But if you want to live to report them, then you should get outside," she insisted, once again pointing down the hall.

"Why?" he asked as the shadow silently crept up behind him.

"Because not all the monsters are gone," she exclaimed. "Look behind you."

He instead stared at her. "I am not falling for the oldest trick in the book."

"Suit yourself. Have a happy afterlife." She didn't stick around to argue. She turned tail—not a real one, the one saving grace of her condition—and ran. Ran past the gaping doors with rooms she'd already stripped. She raced down the hall but, at the intersection, paused.

She didn't hear feet behind her or any screams. Emma cast a glance over her shoulder to see him standing still at the far end, confronting the growing shadow with...a phone? She slapped her pocket and could have groaned as she realized it must have slipped free.

Even from here, she could hear him speak. "...deep in the bowels of the clinic and, as you can see, the things they created still reside, haunting the ruins, preying on the unwary like this living oil slick."

Oh dear. She might not know the true name of the blob, it didn't speak, but was aware it had a taste for flesh. It consumed everything it found, which was great for keeping down the rodent population. Not so great for Oliver, who, with his arrogant attitude, was probably pissing it right off.

Not her problem. She'd told him to get out. He chose not to listen. She turned the corner, took a step, stopped, and sighed.

Flipping around, she ran back, waving her arms. "Shoo, big blobby thing. Don't eat him. If you eat him, people might notice and come looking with flamethrowers."

Oliver cast a glance over his shoulder at her, the camera moving with him. "Is it dangerous?" He saw no claws or fangs.

"Watch out!" was her screamed reply.

The blob heaved, a dark wave rising to flow over Oliver. He had enough sense to jump out of the way, but that was where his intelligence ended.

Gun still in his hand, he fired into the dark morass to little effect. The blob absorbed the bullet, just like it oozed across the floor and walls, determined to smother the man.

Despite the fact he couldn't move his foot—the blob had it—Oliver wasn't done fighting.

He shoved his gun in its holster, rummaged in the pocket of his vest, and emerged with...a saltshaker?

"Fucking nasty leech," he grumbled as he shook the tiny crystals on the blob.

She expected him to get eaten at any moment. Slowly sucked dry like every other unwary victim, only the blob shuddered. Uttered a strange almost screeching noise and withdrew.

But that wasn't enough for the man. Oliver chased it, shaking his salt at it and exclaiming, "How's that, you ungodly creature? There's more where that came from."

Which seemed unlikely, given the amount he'd need to smother the blob was more than he could probably carry.

But he survived to be stupid another day.

To hunt the monsters—*like me.* Which was why she ran back in the direction of the elevator away from the man who'd made it clear she could never hope for a normal life or live among humans again.

CHAPTER FIVE

CHASE THE UNICORN LADY OR THE GIANT LEECH? For a second, Oliver wavered between his choices. On the one hand, the huge blob that wanted to digest him was exactly the kind of monster he'd been looking for in his exposé. And yet, his saltshaker was more than half empty and really pitiful when you considered the amount of crystals he'd need to kill that thing. He'd only brought one along because having had a leech stuck to his dick once before, he preferred salt to holding a lighter to his private parts.

As to why he'd thought to grab it? Call it instinct. Which paid off. The monster had fled.

Given he'd already filmed it, he really should chase down the unicorn lady. For one, the woman who called herself Emma could speak. Questioning her would give him all the juicy details he needed to make people take him seriously. And if they didn't want to listen, then they could stare at her horn.

The thing was rather incredible. Spiraling from her forehead, the tip appearing quite sharp. Imagine the picture she'd make for a viral meme and magazine.

Emma was the story. And she was getting away.

Tucking his phone and saltshaker away, Oliver took off after her, the bouncing beam of his headlight around his neck throwing shadows around, which only heightened his sense of urgency and adrenaline.

He hit the edge of the giant rec room just as she slipped into the open elevator shaft, not even pausing before sliding off the edge.

That kind of fearlessness eluded Oliver, who took a more cautious approach, slowing down when he reached the open elevator doors. He took a moment to shine the light down in to the dark, dark abyss, but it stretched too far for him to truly see anything, the unicorn lady already gone from sight.

"Emma?" He called her name, but there was no reply.

There was, however, a ladder.

Don't do it. He'd gotten his phone back. Discovered the ruins were much more alive than expected. With the footage he already had, he should make it to the surface and upload. Going deeper was insane. Especially if he couldn't find a larger box of salt!

But what of the woman?

If she was running around in here, then how dangerous could it really be? For all he knew, the leech monster would have eaten his clothes and moved on. Yet, she ran.

Maybe she wanted him to chase her so she could lead him into a trap. He should leave.

All the arguing in his head didn't stop him from putting his headlamp back on his forehead then gingerly easing himself into the shaft, his booted foot finding the first rung of the ladder. He was pleased to note it didn't tremble under his weight and seemed firmly anchored.

He began descending, wondering how far down she'd gone. By his calculations there were at least four more floors below him. And she could have exited at any one.

Or not.

At the next floor the doors were jammed shut with a crack barely big enough to shove his hand through. Not something he tried. He'd seen horror movies that showed quite bloodily what happened next.

He kept going down as the chill of this place settled in his bones. The silence was broken only by his own breathing and the *clunk, clunk* of his feet hitting the rungs.

When he stopped moving, he heard nothing. Not a single sign anyone was in here with him.

Either she moved really quietly or she'd exited. At the next floor the doors were partially open, one of them bent and pockmarked as if something had rammed into it over and over. Level Four. The coma patient level. In order to minimize trauma, patients were often put into a deep sleep so that the treatment could be slowly applied, the effects catalogued each step of the way. According to Cerberus, at the time he left the clinic, they had only three coma patients left. All of them moved when they evacuated the clinic.

Possibly a lie given the dents indicated someone from the inside trying to get out.

He kept descending, until he reached level five. According to his recollection of the Cerberus interviews, this floor catered to those who'd woken from their comas. The patients who kept their minds got to live unfettered but secured in their rooms. Prisoners more than patients by all definition.

Was this where Emma used to live? Maybe even still resided?

He hesitated on the ladder. Check out this floor or keep going down to the basement? The lowest level where the worst monsters were kept. Surely a woman with a horn wouldn't have been kept with the normal-looking patients?

He had to wonder. Especially since Cerberus claimed Chimera would have evacuated those on level five. They were considered to be successes. Yet if Emma remained, then didn't that make her one of the dangerous ones from the sixth floor, those they considered unlikely to recover enough to merge with society?

A sound from below decided him. He kept going, more scared than he'd ever admit, yet also excited. This was the type of thing you read about in fantasy books with grand quests. The brave knight would descend into the pit of darkness until he cornered the beast in its lair and slayed it.

Only he didn't really want to kill her. Not like the blob thing and the octopus in the lake. She was too human for him to put a bullet in her brain. Perhaps the horn thing could be fixed? Wouldn't that make for an epic epilogue? The unicorn lady turned back into a human again.

He went down the ladder and was halfway between floors when he heard her cry out from above. "You were supposed to leave."

Looking up, the light on his head illuminated the shaft. He noticed her staring down at him from the fifth level.

"You still haven't given me back my laptop or camera."

Her lips pursed in the dancing beam of his light. "I'm thinking there's not much point in giving them back given you probably won't live long."

"What's that supposed to mean?"

"You should have left when I told you to. Because now you're in really big trouble."

He might have asked what she meant, yet in that moment, something wrapped around his ankle and yanked him off the ladder. The water, when he hit it, was shockingly cold. The cement wall he smacked into? Hard enough to knock him out.

CHAPTER SIX

The stupid light he wore on his forehead slipped underwater and turned into a dull glow. Emma debated walking away.

Let him handle the lake creature. She'd given him so many warnings. Tried to keep him out of danger. But he wouldn't listen.

And why was she even helping him anyhow? He had admitted his plan involved exposing her and all the *monsters,* as he called them.

She should let him drown.

Then she thought of his earnest expression. The passion in him, the life. And while he might lack compassion for her situation, he was wrong.

I'm not a monster.

Which meant she had to at least try and save him. Emma stepped off the edge and hit the water with a splash. She let momentum take her down before she dared to open her eyes. The murky liquid was weirdly lit by his headlamp, enough she could see the tentacle wrapped around Oliver's waist. The curled arm attempted to yank him through flooded elevator doors not open wide enough for something his size.

But the lake monster didn't let that bother it. It slammed the man over and over, hard enough the light fell off his head and drifted down to the bottom, where it sat upon the dead elevator cab.

By its dim light, she kicked and pulled toward Oliver. She would have to free him. Grabbing the rubbery arm, Emma knew better than to try and wrestle. The thing would surpass her strength. She'd have to hurt it, which meant using the only weapon she had.

Still, she hesitated. Waited for the dancing spots but instead saw a last burst of bubbles gush out of Oliver.

He was drowning. She had to stop hesitating.

I have to do this.

Before she could talk herself out of it, she bit her lower lip, lowered her head, and jabbed with her horn. The first poke, lacking strength behind it, bounced off the flesh. The next attempt she rammed it, spearing the tentacle. The reaction proved immediate. The arm released Oliver and retreated through the crack to the sunken sixth floor.

Emma hooked Oliver's sinking body with an arm before stroking up to the surface, shoving his head through first. Emerging second, she sucked in a lungful of air before orienting herself on the ladder that marched down into the water.

The flooding had happened during the explosions. She could only assume some kind of wall between the lake and the lower chamber was cracked open. What she found odd was the water didn't rise to the level of the lake. A good thing or she would have been eking out a very meager existence in the ruins above.

Lugging an unconscious man proved a tad difficult. Not because he was heavy—she was a strong girl now, unlike before when people took advantage of her. A limp Oliver, however, proved unwieldy to move, especially when climbing.

But she managed it, lugging him to the fifth floor and then dragging him through. She continued to drag his body down the hall, leaving a wet streak on buckled tile. She brought him to her home. Ward C, cell number five. The space was untouched when she found it after making her way back to the clinic after the helicopter crash. Lacking outdoor skills and a sense of direction, it took her a bit of time. Winter nipped at her heels the days before she stumbled upon it. The destruction made her cry until she realized it was contained and affected only the topmost levels. She'd never been happier than the moment she hit her floor and stumbled into her familiar space.

My home.

Which she would not share with Oliver.

She eyed him, sopping wet on the floor, then her nice dry bed. "I don't think so," she muttered, reversing course. Heaving him once more, she headed back out into the hall and then proceeded to move a stack of boxes to make him some space that she might place him in the room beside hers. The bed hadn't been used since the evacuation; however, the mattress hadn't yet decayed and only emitted a slightly musty smell when she heaved him onto it.

Oliver hadn't moved since they'd emerged from the water, but he breathed and shivered. His teeth clacked hard enough she wondered if they'd break. She'd already stripped plenty of blankets from other rooms, knowing she had to preserve as much as she could before the rats or nature got to it. Some of the blankets were hung over boxes. She retrieved an armful but hesitated before dumping any on him. His clothes were soaked. They really should be removed. Undressing him, though...

Stop being a ninny.

She tackled his boots first, letting them drop to the floor. Then she went after his socks, which she had to yank off inside out since they were glued to his skin. She gritted her teeth when she dealt with his pants— but left his underwear on. The shirt proved a bit challenging to get over his head and the vest she removed before that, heavy, as if it held stuff. She glanced in the pockets a bit and found a treasure trove of items: multitool with knife and corkscrew, the infamous saltshaker, his phone, even a reel of fishing line. She left everything in its place and concentrated on him once more.

With him mostly denuded, she couldn't help but *see* him before the first sheet went over him. A decent-sized man, he possessed a fit body, lots of lean muscle, a furry chest, and a vee that led to underwear with pizza slices all over it.

Not exactly what she'd expected to see. Didn't most men go for solid-colored briefs?

She shouldn't be paying his undergarment choice any mind. He needed more blankets. She layered them atop his body.

Still, he shivered, a fact that brought a frown, especially since she had no other source of heat.

Yeah, you do.

Much as it pained her, she knew one other option to help warm him up. Before she could think too long about it, she stripped and slid under the blankets, snuggling her warm body to his. Aware of the fact it was skin on skin, hers always hot, his shivering cold.

She draped herself over Oliver to cover as much of his flesh as possible. Hugged him. Put her cheek on his chest and was reassured by the steady beat of his heart. As she relaxed atop him, she couldn't help the spurt of pleasure she got out of being close to someone.

I only had to make sure he was unconscious first. Because if Oliver were awake, he'd surely shove the monster aside in disgust.

The reminder turned down her lips, but she remained atop him as a heating pad. Slowly but surely, his tremors eased, and yet, she didn't move but rather slumbered. For some reason she dreamt of the night the helicopter went down.

Emma woke coughing, her throat tickling and parched, dry and irritated from the heat and smoke she'd breathed in. She opened her eyes and immediately blinked as the acrid air stung them. Jolts of electrical lightning crackled, lighting the area for mere seconds at a time. A nightmarish blink of the eye.

Smoke. Destruction. Even the glow of flames. Crackle, snap, flash.

Blink. It took a moment to realize through the roaring in her ears and the pounding in her skull that she heard more than the hungry licking of flames. She could hear moans, even a soft prayer. "Our Satan, who art in Hell, cursed be thy name. Save your son that I might do your work."

Kind of disturbing but not the most pressing problem. She hung oddly in the harness she'd barely managed to buckle before the helicopter crashed on its side.

"Are you awake?" said a voice from beside her.

"Hope not because this is like a nightmare," she muttered.

"No, nightmare, Una. We're in big trouble. We need to get out of this thing before it blows."

Her sluggish brain put his words together with the other signs of danger: fire, fuel... Uh-oh.

The realization snapped some focus back into her, and she ran her hands over the harness looking for the clip. Click. It took falling for her to realize she should have grabbed hold of something. Instead, she landed on the still sleeping Barry. At least she hoped he was sleeping and not dead.

She scrambled away from him and stood awkwardly. Now what?

"Let me loosssse." The hissed request came from the guy seated beside her. Jacob was fully bound, like everyone else, but awake. Aware.

"Um, yeah. Give me a second," she said, looking around for a way to reach him.

"Don't really have a second, Una."

"My name is Emma."

"Mine will be barbecue if you don't get me out of this contraption."

She ended up grabbing hold of her dangling harness, hauling herself up, and then hooking one arm that the other might deal with the clips holding him in place. Poor Barry got used as a landing pillow again and grunted. She leaped down beside Jacob and began undoing the buckles of his straightjacket.

"Faster, Unicorn girl. It's getting hot in here."

Hot and smoky.

The moment his arms were free, Jacob removed the rest of the constraints and leapt for the door at the rear of the chopper. Opening it brought a whiff of fresh air.

And freedom.

He stood framed in the doorway. "Coming, Una?"

"Shouldn't we help the others?" She glanced at their prone bodies.

His gaze followed hers, saw them helpless and in need of their aid, yet he managed to say, "When it comes to survival, it's every man for themselves." Then he left.

Left while the flames got hotter, the smoke thicker.

Emma might have followed except... She wasn't an asshole. Which was why she began tackling those caught on the bottom first. Unhooking them and tossing them out the back, thankful for her extra strength. She'd worry about their cocooning restraints later—if she had a later.

She didn't have much time. In the movies, explosions happened quickly.

It turned out Jacob wasn't the only one who'd regained consciousness. She came across another person who was awake.

Xiu watched with those wide-open freaky white eyes. "I can help."

The woman might appear blind, but she could unbuckle faster than Emma. She helped get those who were still breathing unhooked, making Emma's job the one of pack unicorn carrying them out to the safer ground outside.

Although, by the time they reached the last one, it appeared they needn't hurry. The flames had sputtered out, and yet they continued to work until every living body was outside.

Janice, another one who'd woken, didn't stick around, claiming, "They'll probably send a search party to round us up."

Sounded good to Emma. Which was why, when the others woke, they found her sitting atop the wreckage watching the sky.

They called her deluded and suffering from Stockholm syndrome when she insisted she wanted to stay and be rescued. They laughed when she said she missed the comfort of her room at the clinic. All of them ran away and left her behind.

By the third day of waiting, her belly hungry and miserable with damp and cold, she realized no one was coming. She moved from the wreckage and began wandering the mountain range and forests. Scavenging for the fall berries that were overripe and few. Freezing at night when the temperature dropped. Running into a few of the others who escaped—not situations that ended well.

It took her a while to find her way home, only to discover a ruin. The sight of the rubble had her crying for days. She might have died staring at it in despair, but as winter crept in, she ran out of places to huddle and stay warm. With nothing left to lose, she dared to enter the ruins and discovered the damage was mostly on the surface. She made it down into the belly of the clinic and found out she wasn't alone.

It wasn't as reassuring as you'd expect. The night she woke to something heavy on her she held her breath lest she make a sound.

Don't say a word or he'll hit you.

That was the best way to handle it. Except, she wasn't that scared girl anymore. She didn't have to say yes. She could say no, and if he didn't listen, she. Would. Roar.

"Get off me."

"Pretttttty," *the thing hissed, tearing at her clothes.*

"No." *She shoved at the heavier body.* "No!"

"What the hell?"

The voice was a different one, and as she stared at the face above her, it changed, turned into Oliver, and he was under her, confusion in his face...

...because she was awake and shoving at him.

"Oliver?" she queried.

"Who else would I be?" Said in a grumpy tone.

"How do you feel?" Because, from her perspective atop him, he felt mighty fine. Warm, too. She squirmed against him, and his body reacted in a way that had her freezing.

"Emma, what the fuck is going on? Why are you naked on top of me?"

"To warm you up. You fell in the water."

"Fell?" He snorted. "That octopus from the lake tried to kill me."

"It did."

"Don't tell me you saved me again." Said with a groan.

"Okay."

"Okay what?"

"You told me not to tell you," she said in absolute innocence.

"Ha. Ha. Not funny. Who helped you get me into this bed?"

"No one."

It took him a moment before he snapped out, "Do all the Chimera monsters get super strength?"

The reminder of his feelings about her brought a frown. "That's not a nice thing to say."

He sighed. "No, it wasn't. I'm sorry. Just a little out of sorts. This is twice today I've almost died."

"Three if you count the blob."

"Thanks for reminding me," was the dry retort.

Her lips curved into a smile she knew he couldn't see in the dark. "You're welcome."

"How long was I unconscious?"

She shrugged. "I don't exactly keep time down here."

"Here being?"

"Fifth floor."

"Is that where you live?"

Again, she gave a subtle squirm of her body that might have brushed parts it shouldn't have. "Yes." No point in denying it.

"Doesn't it get lonely?"

"Very." Which might be why the erection he couldn't hide didn't send her running.

"Does anyone else live here?"

Was he seriously interrogating her?

"According to you, monsters."

"How many?"

"Depends on the day. Some of them come and go. Others, like the blob, never leave."

"Did you ever try and leave?"

She shook her head, the strands of it whipping his face.

"Why not leave the mountains?"

"And go where? Do what? It's not like I can hide my horn with a wig or a hat."

"You could have it removed."

How to explain it always came back? It was as if her body considered it an essential limb. No matter how many times it got trimmed, by the next morning, a nub returned. Within a week, it measured several inches long.

"What's the point? I'll never be normal."

"So you do regret getting the cure?"

"No. It's still better than dying. But I wish the clinic was still here."

"Why would you want to be a prisoner to those evil doctors?" he asked, sounding flabbergasted.

"Because they were nice to me."

"They experimented on you." He sounded mad.

"I get it. You don't understand," she huffed. "But put yourself in someone else's shoes. Imagine you've been told you're dying. You're already in pain. And it's going to get worse. You're all alone. You have no one to hold your hand. No one to lie and say shit will get better. You have only pain and misery to look forward to, and certain death. Then along comes a guy who says, hey, I know someone who can help you."

"Chimera," he said with a sneer.

"Yes, Dr. Chimera. A man who deserves praise, not your disdain. He saved my life when he didn't have to. He could have left me dying in that hospital. Could have walked away and never cured a damned person, but because of him, so many of us got a second chance."

"How can you call this a life? You're living in ruins with things that don't even look human anymore."

"Because people like you think I shouldn't exist," Emma blurted out. Then, because she couldn't stand to be close to a man who thought so little of her, she shoved away, rolled right out of the bed. "Your clothes are drying on a chair," she said before fleeing the room.

As if running away would get rid of him. His words followed her, ensuring that she felt more alone than ever.

CHAPTER SEVEN

Oliver regretted the harshness of his words the moment the warm naked body slipped away. What kind of idiot did that?

The kind that remained snug under the covers. He felt perfectly hot at the moment, so it wasn't like he needed her. However, he did feel like a heel.

He'd deliberately insulted her. Called her a monster. Mostly to keep himself in check, but it didn't work. The erection remained, and he wanted to touch her something fierce. He managed to keep his hands to himself. Given her naked body atop his was the problem, he needed her off because she hadn't seemed inclined to move on her own.

So he insulted her until she finally got the point. He hurt her and immediately wanted to apologize. Good thing she left before he did. He was hoping her closeness didn't infect him with what she had. Cerberus had assured him they weren't contagious, and yet, Oliver hadn't felt like himself since meeting her. She must have done something to him!

A thought to make even him ashamed. The woman had risked herself saving him. Told him of her sad past. Gave him a glimpse of her loneliness.

And he made it worse.

So much for thanking her for not letting him die. Last he recalled his lungs were about to burst from a lack of air and the cold bite of the water as the octopus came back for round two.

He lived. A little bit bruised, he noticed as he began to move. His body was sore in a few places but a better alternative than being digested by the calamari he usually preferred breaded on a plate.

Because Emma saved him.

A monster to the rescue, who'd not only ripped Oliver from the clutches of another monster but somehow carried him to safety. Then got naked with him to make sure he didn't die of hypothermia.

God, I am such a dick.

He owed her his gratitude and an apology, and he'd give it to her if he could ever find his way in the dark. There wasn't a smidgen of light in this place. Just pure black.

How did she handle it?

Oliver didn't think he could live in absolute darkness. Not seeing meant he tensed, wondering how close the walls leaned in on him. What if danger lurked? He wouldn't see it coming.

"Emma?" He said her name, wondering if she'd remained close by.

A reply wasn't forthcoming. Not from her or anything else, but how could he be sure he was alone?

The blob would love to catch him unaware. A thought that should have galvanized and yet froze him in his bed. How emasculating that he feared putting his foot on the floor.

He'd never exactly gotten over his fear of the monster hiding under the bed. In some cases, though— as he'd learned on his trip to Moscow to unearth a smuggling scheme—humans were the ones hiding.

Did the ceiling bow overhead? Was he perhaps just a moment away from triggering a collapse?

So many things could go wrong if he got out of this warm bed. Yet staying wasn't a guarantee.

Oliver knew he lay in a bed because he could feel it under him, the mattress covered in fabric, the weight of blankets over him part of how he remained snug. Listening, he heard nothing, not even an electrical hum or the drip of water. The dead silence of a ruin long abandoned—by normal people.

Are you going to stay hiding under the sheets until the monsters come to get you?

No. Time to get moving. Oliver sat up, the blankets falling from his upper body. The cold air, damp on his skin, brought a shiver. He tucked the sheet tight, pulling at it until he could wrap it toga style around his body. Sat on the edge of the bed, dangling his feet, wishing he could see.

How far was the floor? How much space under the bed? Did he hear something breathing? He paused to listen.

Nope. Just his own fear coming to life.

Before running away, Emma had said something about his clothes being nearby to dry. Doubtful about the dry part, but if he could find his vest, then he might be able to create some light. He'd also have access to a knife.

Before he could talk himself out of it, he pushed to stand. The concrete pressed coldly against the soles of his bare feet. Nothing grabbed ahold of his ankles.

A good sign.

Oliver reached out to see if he could touch anything. He waved his hands, leaning forward until he hit the edges of a cardboard box that had gotten soft and damp. With something to orient him, he felt his way along until he bumped into something that rattled. More groping led him to touching damp fabric, the canvas familiar, as were the cargo-style pockets. Pants. More groping led to his shirt as well, also clammy to the touch. He left them there and kept touching and shuffling slowly until he bumped into a stack of boxes. Lain across them, his goal.

He felt the pockets of his vest, looking for a specific one. His hand closed around it, and he uttered an "Aha" as he pulled it free. It took two hands to crack it.

The glow stick proved too bright in the pitch-black, and he blinked as it flared to life. Then blinked again as he took stock around him.

He was in some kind of room. The bed and the area around it being the only spots free of boxes and heaps of fabric.

Clothes, he realized as he began to wander the stacks. Blankets. Towels. In the boxes, food supplies. Canned goods. A whole box full of microwave bags of popcorn. A variety of items left behind after the explosion and squirreled away.

This was Emma's stash he realized. It saddened him as he realized she'd obviously moved all these things to a secure place lest they spoil. The sadder part was the dampness would probably destroy them anyhow.

Waving his glow wand back in the direction of the bed, he noticed the thick pile of blankets and wondered if this was where she slept.

Would she come back?

He probably should dress before that happened. Just not in his wet clothes. He rummaged through the piles, managing to find menswear amongst the apparel, big sweatshirts and track pants, a bit cold and damp initially, but after shivering a few minutes, he got warm again. Socks also proved easy to find, but there were no boots or shoes in his size other than his soggy pair. He put on a second pair of socks instead. He found his tool belt. Minus the gun and knife.

All his weaponry appeared lost—or taken. His salt-shaker had water inside, the remaining crystals a solid hunk. Not the most auspicious of things. He'd have to stay away from leeching puddles and octopus arms.

For some reason he snorted. Who would have thought he'd ever have to worry about that kind of shit?

His phone had actually survived the dunking, the waterproof casing worth the price tag. It just didn't have any signal this deep in the ruined clinic. He bundled his things, including his boots and vest, and put them in a drawstring bag that used to hold a bunch of silverware. He'd dumped the forks and spoons and knives on the bed, wincing at the noise it made. He stuffed his things in the bag and then grabbed a fork for good measure.

Better than a spoon if he had to jab something.

Slinging the string bag on his back, he exited out the only door in the room, the hinges silent as it opened. A relief because he'd half expected to be locked in. He found himself in a hall.

A wave of his glowing wand showed numbers on the wall beside each door, much like a cellblock. Which brought another wave of compassion he wouldn't have expected.

Yes, those Chimera changed were monsters, but they weren't willing ones. They were kept prisoner to the follies of a madman. Victims that never had a choice.

That line of thinking made his jaw tighten. He couldn't start feeling sorry for them now. They were a blight on mankind. A spreading virus that could change the face of humanity forever. They had to be eradicated now, before it was too late.

You gonna kill them yourself? his conscience

taunted. It was one thing to take down a charging bear or an animal to feed himself. Could he kill in cold blood?

That octopus thing? No problem. Even that puddle of goo if he had a pile of salt to shake. But even he wasn't cold enough to shoot the unicorn lady.

Thing was he knew there were people out there who would. All it would take was him posting about her existence and this place would be overrun with morons bearing guns. He'd be an accomplice to murder.

What if they didn't kill her, though? What if instead they took her prisoner? Made her a centerpiece in a freak show? Or worse.

How could he know what the right thing was? Before the valley, it seemed so black and white. Monsters evil. Pharmaceutical company and its plans, really evil. Humanity...in need of saving.

But wasn't Emma human too? Didn't she deserve his help?

He tried to ignore the war inside his head. He shoved everything out and stepped into the hallway with its many doors. All closed. He had a choice—make his way to the surface with haste or...

Open the door across from him apparently. He peeked in and saw the same scenario as the room he'd left. A bed and some boxes strewn with more fabric. The room beside it, though, had him recoiling. Upon opening it, he noticed the destruction. The mattress torn to shreds. The bare furniture smashed and destroyed. As he stepped farther into the room, a sudden horrified realization hit him as he noticed the walls by the exit and the inside of the door itself. Scratched. Dented. Painted in brown streaks that could only be dried blood.

"Jesus fucking Christ. They left one here alive."

"More than one," said a soft voice.

He cast a glance over his shoulder to see Emma peeked around the edge of the doorframe, the tip of her horn appearing first.

"Where's the body?" he asked because he didn't see one anywhere.

"I removed it," she admitted. "I burned all the ones I found."

The very idea that this petite woman had done such a thing surprised. "Why?"

Her shoulders rolled in a shrug. "Because I didn't want the rodents and bugs to get them. I don't know how impervious to disease I am and because—" She paused chewing her lower lip. "They didn't get the chance and dignity they deserved in life, so I gave them one in death."

A noble gesture. For a monster. Who in that moment just seemed lost and alone.

Which reminded him. "I was a dick when I woke, and you didn't deserve it. Especially since you saved me from dying. Thank you."

She ducked her head, her hair forming a curtain across her face that only served to highlight the horn. "You're welcome, I guess."

"Regretting your decision?"

"Maybe a little." She sighed. "It would have probably been better to let you drown on level six. Alive, you'll only cause trouble."

"What makes you say that?" he asked.

Her head lifted, and he saw the glow of her eyes through the skeins of hair. "You're here to expose the clinic. To put an end to me and everyone Chimera touched."

He thought about lying, but something in her gaze stopped him. He owed this woman his life. The least he could do was give her the truth.

"What happened here was wrong."

"According to who? You?"

He snorted. "Are you seriously going to argue? All right then, it's wrong according to everything. Laws. Human rights. Common decency."

Her turn to make a scoffing noise. "Please. Dr. Chimera and his staff were angels of mercy. If it weren't for them, I and so many others would be feeding the worms right now."

"The doctors here preyed on the downtrodden."

"They gave a chance to those of us who never had one," she retorted hotly, facing him full on. "How dare you judge what they did here without recognizing the good."

"Where's the good in the creation of monsters?"

"Am I a monster?" she asked him point-blank.

The right answer stared him in the face. He wanted to shout, "Have you looked in a mirror, lady?"

Yet, he held back. Monsters didn't put themselves in danger saving others. They didn't care about the dignity of the dead. "You are the exception, I think. Everything else I've encountered so far has only proven me right."

"Meaning what?" She arched a brow. "Is that what you're really after? The eradication of what you deem monsters? And you would call Dr. Chimera the villain. He at least attempted to improve our lives. Kept us sheltered. Protected."

"Until he abandoned you and killed those he left behind."

Her lips flattened. "He tried to save most of us."

"He didn't save you."

Her chin lifted. "He tried, but the helicopter I was on crashed."

"I can't believe you're making excuses for him after what he did."

"I can't believe you would condemn without knowing the full story."

"I know enough thanks to Dr. Cerberus." He ran his mouth a little too much.

Her eyes widened. "You've seen him?"

He almost denied it, but the truth came out instead. "Yes, I've seen him. Plenty of times. He's the reason I'm here."

"What have you done to him?" she exclaimed. "You better not have hurt him. He was one of the nicest doctors."

"Me, hurt him? Have you seen the guy?" He

paused and frowned. "I guess you haven't recently. He's not the man you remember." He was no longer a man at all.

"What of Dr. Chimera? Have you seen him, too?"

"That prick is still missing. But if he's out there, he will be found. People are looking for him."

"I hope they never find him," she pertly replied before turning on her heel and leaving.

"How deluded are you?" he asked, following her into the hall, barely able to see her in the faint glow of his stick.

"I could ask the same of you. Although, in your case, it's more that you're close minded. Dr. Chimera might have been using science in a way the world hasn't yet grasped or approved, but you seem to be determined to ignore the fact he cured people."

"A cure shouldn't change what a person is."

"By your definition." She cast a glance over her shoulder. "And maybe that's why there are still so many illnesses in the world. Do you know, once upon a time, doctors used leeches to bleed their patients? Nor did they sterilize equipment."

"Because they didn't know any better."

Her lips curved into a smile. "Exactly."

"You can't equate the mixing of animal DNA with human to a better medical understanding."

"Have you ever taken antibiotics?"

"Who hasn't?"

"Yet they aren't natural. Neither is most pain medicine."

"Marijuana is natural."

"And it's classified as a dangerous drug in most countries. Funny thing, that. There are things in the world that could help people and save lives, yet they're forbidden. Why is that, do you think?"

Was he seriously having a debate five stories underground with a woman who thought a psychopath should get a free pass experimenting with humans? He was, and it engaged his mind in a way he'd never imagined. Especially since he saw where her query led. And it led to the very thing he was also fighting against.

"The big pharmaceutical companies aren't interested in cures. Especially cheap and easy ones." Because how else would they make their profit selling overpriced medicine?

For a long time now, the conspiracy theorists claimed there was a cure for cancer and other diseases. He knew for a fact they were right. Problem was there was no money to be made in a cure.

"Tell me," Emma said. "If you suddenly found out tomorrow you had an incurable brain tumor, that you could either die within three months or try something experimental, something that you knew might still kill you but if it didn't, would let you live, what would you choose?"

The self-righteous lie sat on the tip of his tongue. *I'd rather die than become a monster.* Yet...was that really true? If he were faced with a life or death situation, would he feel differently?

She opened a door and entered a space that soon

filled with light. Following her, he paused as he realized she'd taken him to her room, the one she lived in. It was easy to discern, given the posters on the wall, some simple images torn from magazines, others drawn in highlighter and pen. Along one wall paperbacks were stacked, hundreds of them. Light illuminated every corner, and he frowned.

"I thought there was no electricity here."

She cast him a look over her shoulder. "There isn't. But there is plenty of cooking oil." She pulled off a lampshade to show him the jar filled with amber fluid, the strip of fabric that formed a wick within holding the flame.

"Aren't you worried about the smoke?"

"I keep my door open, and while the generators don't circulate the air, the vents do still draw." She pointed overhead.

"Wouldn't it be easier to just go back to civilization?"

"Weren't you the one who said I couldn't? I know what they'll do to me if I ever go back."

"So your plan is to live here forever?"

A sad expression pulled down her lips. "I don't have much of a choice."

"Because Chimera screwed you."

That brought the fierceness back to her face. "He was helping me, unlike everyone else in my life. And then because someone—like you probably—tried to take it away, he had to leave. But I'm hoping he'll come back."

"So he can finish the job?" he said with a sneer.

"So I can feel normal again," she snapped. "It's because of intolerant people like you that I have to hide in this ruin. But you don't understand what that's like. Look at you. Handsome. Intelligent. Rich, too, I'll bet because your equipment sure isn't cheap. Thinking you're better than me. Better than everyone who doesn't agree with you."

The handsome part pleased him. Even the mention he was bright. But the rest— "You make me sound like an asshole when I'm not."

"And you keep making me out to be a monster when I'm not," she huffed.

"You could probably get that fixed," he said, pointing to the horn in the room.

"What if I don't want to?" The hot retort held a glare.

Her query boggled the mind. "Why wouldn't you?"

"Because, for the first time in my life, I'm someone special. I'm not just Emma Kylie Baker. I'm a freakin' unicorn."

CHAPTER EIGHT

Chest heaving with emotion, Emma couldn't believe she'd just blurted that out. She'd never dared say it aloud. Yet it was true. For all that the horn meant she had to hide, it made her special.

One of a kind. A unicorn.

It was also what made Oliver eye her with a hint of disgust. At least at first. Now she didn't know what he felt when he looked at her, but he seemed very set in his plan to reveal her existence and eradicate it.

And if she couldn't convince him she was worth saving, a man she'd not harmed, a man she'd saved, then how could she convince the world?

"You are not a unicorn." He rolled his eyes. "You're a lady with a bony protuberance. It doesn't make you special."

"Says you. My doctors disagree." Dr. Sphinx might have been a lot of things—including maggot food in the woods—but she never doubted Sphinx thought she was special compared to the other patients. She knew not all of them got the treats she did. None of the others got to decorate their room or have their own television.

As to the blackouts—the ones that started with black dancing spots—where she seemed to lose a few days? According to Sphinx, she sometimes fell into a coma-like sleep. He'd even shown her footage. Which, in retrospect, could have been taken at any time. She'd never suspected subterfuge until that moment on the helicopter.

"Why were you being treated?" Oliver asked. "Why did they recruit you into their program?"

"Because I was sick, obviously." At his continued stare, she sighed. "You want the whole dirty truth? Fine. But I warn you, it's not pretty. I was born with fetal alcohol syndrome and addicted to heroin. Spent the first few weeks of my life in the hospital. Then a few more in the care of foster parents, according to my file." She sat down heavily on the comfy club chair Dr. Sphinx had brought her, the flowered pattern worn but bright. "For some reason, child services thought it was a bright idea to give me back into the loving care of my drug-addicted mother. The extra welfare money meant Mama could get high even more often. The only reason I survived because of a neighbor." But when Clarice had to move, having gotten herself a job that made her ineligible for the subsidized housing, there went the warm hugs and the food she shared from her meager supply.

A frown knit his brow. "Sounds like you had a rough childhood."

"Rough childhood. Abusive teen years. Which didn't stop even when I moved out. There were times I thought I had victim tattooed on my forehead. I never seemed to be able to escape the life I was born into. And eventually, it tried to kill me."

Actually, what really happened was Manny—the boyfriend of the day—tried to kill her. He'd started out treating her so nice when she met him at rehab for the families of drug addicts. They left, clean and determined to give it a shot. Only, he fell off the wagon.

The last beating he gave her put her in the hospital with a few broken ribs where the x-rays revealed it and a mammogram confirmed it.

"I had cancer in both my breasts. Already spread to my lymph nodes and my lungs. Turned out my cough wasn't because of the nicotine I inhaled growing up but because I was riddled with cancer. Then, because I was a lost cause with no insurance, I was basically told I might as well go home and prepare to die."

"Hospitals can't kick you out for no insurance."

"Can't and don't are two different things. It does happen, more than is perhaps admitted. And who can blame them? Why waste a bed on a dying woman whose only contribution to the world was not procreating?" Her words held a bitterness to them. She'd long ago decided to never have children. She wouldn't subject a child to the upbringing she suffered.

"How did Chimera find you?"

She shrugged. "I don't know. Don't really care. Suffice it to say, his lawyer showed up on my doorstep." Which, at that time, was an alley near her last true residence. Manny, the shitty boyfriend, replaced her the moment he realized she wouldn't be around much longer. "He told me I had a chance to live and it wouldn't cost me a thing."

"Except your humanity."

At that she sneered. "Humanity never gave a damn about the men who thought they could use me. Humanity wasn't there when I was coughing up blood, my belly a knot of pain from hunger and the cancer. But the Chimaeram Clinic was. They took away my pain by curing my cancer. For the first time in my life, I'm healthy. I didn't even realize how much my fucked-up birth and upbringing hurt until all that pain was gone. And now you think you can stand there and tell me I made the wrong choice?" She shook her head. "I would make that same choice again and again. I would even do it if I grew a tail or turned into a damned unicorn with hooves and all."

"Unicorns are cute creatures, I'll grant you that, but can you say the same of that leech thing upstairs? Or the tentacle monster in the basement?"

"You call them monsters because they don't look like you."

"I call them monsters because they tried to kill me."

"You kill." Best not to think of the spots that sometimes preceded the scent of copper.

"No, I don't," he huffed, trying to act indignant.

"Really? Because I saw the traps you set. You eat meat."

"Small game, which isn't the same—"

"As what? You hunt to eat."

"I don't hunt people, though."

"Neither are they. You keep saying the others are not human anymore, which means you're just meat to them." She smiled. Not a very nice smile, which was at odds with how she used to be. In that respect he was right. The treatment did change her. It made her able to speak out and stand up for herself.

Ain't no one putting me in a corner. Not anymore.

"I can't believe you just said that. That's sick." He fiddled with his phone, looking intently at the screen and tapping it.

She frowned. "What are you doing?"

"Proving that even the most human appearing of you can't be trusted."

"You were taping me?" she gasped.

He at least had the grace to look sheepish. "You knew I came here looking for evidence."

"I didn't give you permission to use my words. Or my face. Hand it over."

He shook his head and tucked it into his pocket. "I'm sorry, but I can't keep you or this place a secret. The world has a right to know. Don't worry, I'll make sure you get the help you need. You're not like the other monsters. We can save you."

"How dare you!" She sprang from her chair, every

inch of her bristling. "Hand it over now." She held out her hand.

"No." He backed away, and she stalked him.

"I can't let you leave with it."

Rather than reply, he gave her one last long stare and then bolted.

Seriously?

Did he not grasp she knew this place inside and out?

The idiot ran for the elevator shaft, and she let him. With luck, he'd lose his grip and fall, taking care of the problem for her.

Because he really didn't want her catching up to him, not with the rage rising and the black spots dancing.

That never ended well.

At least for the person pissing her off. She might want to bring a rag to wipe her horn.

CHAPTER NINE

OLIVER UNDERSTOOD THE MOMENT HE RAN HE PUT himself at a disadvantage. He didn't know this place like Emma did, nor did he have monster strength.

Good thing she is strong or you'd be dead.

His damned conscience wouldn't stop nagging him. It took issue with the fact he'd hurt her. Not physically, but he'd seen the betrayal in her expression as she realized their entire conversation was taped.

It was an asshole thing to do, and quite honestly, the first three-quarters of the conversation almost destroyed his entire reason for making sure the monsters were destroyed. Then she called humans meat.

Who the fuck did that?

Monsters did. Which was why he bolted with the evidence rather than hand it over. She could threaten, but he didn't think she would actually hurt him.

He hit the opening for the elevator shaft and

climbed through, casting a wary glance down. Knowing what lay below meant he couldn't afford to slip. With the glow stick tucked between his teeth lighting his way, he began to climb, quickly reaching the fourth floor, making it almost to the second when he saw it, a sheet of black ooze creeping down.

"Are you fucking kidding me?" He glanced down and saw the round oval of her face coming up behind him. Caught between a horn and a blood-sucking place.

Luckily, he was also level with some kind of ventilation shaft. He wiggled into it, army-man crawling in the dusty space, his breath heaving hotly as he moved, wondering if he'd made a mistake. There was no room to turn around. No escape if something came at him from the front. No slowing down in case he was caught at the back.

At a fork in the shaft, he went upward, not far, but enough that when he saw a grill, he kicked it out and spilled into a corridor on the third level. Surely that elevator wasn't the only exit? He bolted for the far end of the hall, noticing the long line of windows looking into ancient labs. Labs he could oddly see. His step slowed as he realized some of the instruments glowed as if painted with phosphorescence.

Or slimed by some new kind of monster.

Oliver kept moving, his fast walk turning once more into a run, especially when he heard a clang behind him. He didn't bother to look. Looking slowed a person down. Besides, he didn't really want to know what chased him. An angry unicorn? An oil slick? Or something worse?

And all I've got is a fork to stab it with.

The far end of the hall appeared to be a solid wall of stone with a dead control panel beside it.

"Dammit!" He kicked the dead end and felt something move. He stared at the stone façade and noticed a straight edge. A few of them, actually, forming a rectangle in the wall.

He heaved and shoved and gaped as the wall moved, revealing a secret passage. He slid into a new hallway lined with doors, all of them shut and padlocked. The stench in this place unbelievable—and much like a plague hospital in a South American jungle he'd once visited for a story. He'd wager there was death behind those doors, but he didn't have time to check. He ran to the far end, the door there giving at his push.

He entered another abandoned lab and thought he'd hit a dead end until the glow stick he waved around showed a welcome sight. Grimy elevator doors, smaller ones, but they had to lead somewhere. His breath came in ragged gasps as he grabbed at the doors and tried to wedge them apart.

Not even a tiny budge. He glanced around, convinced at any moment someone would jump in. The silence made every harsh breath too loud. A metal ruler left lying on a counter had just the right thickness to be wedged into the crack of the elevator doors. It broke before he'd managed to pry the doors an inch.

An inch proved enough room to jam something bigger in the slit, the leg of a metal stool that made an awful noise—*Wham. Wham*—when he separated it from the seat by slamming it on the floor, his gaze still trained on the doors.

Nothing came seeking the source of the noise, and with the broken leg, he heaved the doors wide enough to squeeze through and almost fall. He held on with the tips of his fingers as a foot dangled in dead space. There was a ladder set within the shaft, and he began climbing it, his muscles screaming at him to take a break.

His heart screaming at him he was going to die of a heart attack.

But he kept going. Time enough to rest when he made it back to the surface.

Somehow, he found the strength to climb and kept climbing even when he lost his grip on the glow stick. There was no going back. He kept going until his hands hit a blockage.

"Shit," he cursed. Now what? He glanced down, wondering if he should go down a level, pry open a new set of doors, but a sound from below decided him.

He had to get out. He ran his hands over the debris. Parts of it seemed loose. He yanked at some drywall, and it went tumbling. He almost shouted a warning in case Emma still followed.

I thought you wanted to get away from her.

Away, yes, but he didn't actually want to see her harmed.

He kept pulling and tugging at the precarious rubble. Hope filled him when a sliver of light poked through. He yanked and pummeled some more at the wreckage. Cursed as dust silted into his eyes. He blinked through gritty tears and kept working at the pile until he was rewarded with more than a trickle of daylight. Shoving his shoulder into a chunk of concrete sent it sailing down, and the shaft illuminated.

Something hissed, and the air filled with an obnoxious smell. A glance downward had Oliver gulping. The oil slick hung only a rung below his foot. It shriveled in the light, faint smoke rising from its skin.

Much like a vampire, it fled the light of day, quickly oozing back down the ladder. One less thing to worry about. Oliver gladly went for the sunlight, wiggling through the hole he'd made, hoping he didn't upset the ruins too much. He'd hate to go plummeting after making it this far.

He eventually made it out and lay across a slanted hunk of concrete, breathing hard.

I did it. Made it to the surface alive. With the evidence.

"Give it." Emma's voice didn't come from the hole he'd escaped but farther away.

He sat up and glanced over the rubble. He was closer to the edge of it than expected, and Emma stood just beyond it, arms crossed, fully illuminated in the daylight. For a moment he was stunned.

He'd noticed her as a woman before. Her petite frame shapely, her features quite lovely. Her horn quite noticeable. It was even more noticeable now, glittering as if covered in bling. And her eyes glowed like diamonds.

"You know I can't do that, Emma. But I promise I'll get you help." He pulled out his phone and began tapping, cursing as the weak signal threatened to cut out. He needed to get the video out there.

"Bad." A single word growled as if by a mouth that had forgotten how to form consonants.

A glance over at Emma meant he saw her lower her horn and rub her foot on the ground.

His eyes widened. "Emma, what are you doing?" Surely, she wasn't about to charge him?

She did, arms and legs pumping, her head down and the tip of it pointing the way.

"Emma, no, you'll hurt yourself," he yelled.

It didn't slow her one bit. He winced in anticipation of the painful impact, when her body suddenly stopped running and arched. She let out a sound, "Aaah," before crumpling to the ground.

"Emma?" He stood and stared with incomprehension. Had she fainted?

It was then the sound penetrated. An engine revved. He whirled on his slab and noticed figures jogging across the field, guns in their hands, and beyond them was a helicopter, black and unmarked, its rotors slowly moving, gaining power.

Ah shit. The government had sent some goons. He glanced at his phone. The upload bar showed the video at sixty-three percent.

"Arms where we can see them!" a big dude with a long duster shouted, leading the way with his weapon pointed out.

"It's okay. I'm not one of them," Oliver announced and added, "I'm human." He began jumping from slab to leaning slab, hands up, one clutching his phone. Here was to hoping his acrobatics to get off the rubble didn't disconnect his signal.

"Stop moving and state your name," barked the dark-haired fellow, taking a stance while a golden-haired man with empty hands and a dark-skinned woman with two guns flanked him.

He froze. "Name is Oliver Taylor. I'm—" He paused as his mind sought for a quick answer that didn't involve the truth. "On vacation."

"Here?" queried the leader of the group.

"I like hiking. In mountains. You find really cool shit." He kept his hands raised and didn't dare look at his phone.

"What's he got in his hand?" The woman had noticed, damn it.

"Fuck he's got a phone," muttered the blond fellow whose hair tufted Wolverine style.

"You better not be calling for backup," grumbled the duster fellow. "Idiot. Drop the phone."

He could only hope the video made it. The cell hit the ground face down, hiding the screen. "I feel like I should mention that my travel plans are well known—"

"Doubtful," muttered the woman.

"—and that it's not like this place is a secret."

"Actually, it is. Which means someone opened their mouth and told you its location." The dark-haired fellow glowered.

"Does this mean we can't just kill him and dump his body?" The woman's cold, flat stare was scarier than the guns she held. He'd have to remember that when he wrote this chapter for the book. If he lived long enough to type it.

"Hold on. You can't kill me. People will notice."

"And? It's not like they'll know what happened."

The leader had a point.

"Who are you? Government? Company boys? Mercs?"

"How about none of the above? Now shut it for a minute while I talk to my team." The leader kept his eyes on Oliver but addressed his companions. "Jayda, check on Emma. Luke, circle around the ruins and see if you can detect anyone else."

"Are you looking for more of the monsters?" Oliver asked, taking a chance and doing one final leap to the ground.

The man's jaw tightened, but he didn't shoot. "You seen any?"

No point in hiding them. Especially given the danger they posed. "There's some giant octopus in the lake. And a vampire oil patch that moves around inside. Other than that, no one but Emma." He shrugged. "But I've only been here like two days. For all I know there could be lots more."

"Who else knows you're here?"

Tricky question because, technically, no one did, but replying that way might see him buried in the ruins. "My family. I've been texting them and sending videos of my travels."

"Sure, you have. You came here alone." More a statement than query. The guy smirked. "Hiking for pleasure my ass. What do you know about the Chimaeram Clinic?"

Oliver countered with, "What do you know?" More than ever he was thinking this group might be military special ops.

"You seriously think you can ask questions? Jesus, you've got balls. And I don't have time for this shit. You're coming with us."

Oliver shook his head. "I don't think so. I know my rights. You can't detain me."

"Aw, isn't that cute. He thinks he has rights," said by a sarcastic Jayda, who had Emma slung across her shoulders and was headed toward the helicopter.

The sight had Oliver blurting out, "Where are you taking her?"

Jayda whirled and walked backwards so she could toss him a smirk. "Bringing her somewhere safer than here."

"Are you going to kill her?"

"Would it matter?" Jayda asked, pausing for his reply.

"Oh, for fuck's sake," groaned the dark-haired one. "I thought we were here looking for survivors."

"And looks like we found the most viable ones. The

main tracks leading in and out from the ruins belong to her," announced Luke, jogging up to join them. "Second fresher set also enter. His, I'll bet." The fellow got a tad too close for Oliver's comfort and gave a big sniff.

Which was weird enough, but the green glow in the guy's eyes?

Oliver's stomach sank. "You're not working for the government, are you?"

Before Oliver could fully grasp and enjoy the shit he'd managed to fall in, the grim-faced fellow raised his gun and shot him. The last thing Oliver saw was the guy's grin.

"No. We're the monsters you're looking for."

CHAPTER TEN

EMMA WOKE IN A BED. NOT HER BED IN THE clinic, she might add. The bleach in the sheets tickled her nose. And was that...? She smelled bacon!

Which wasn't something she usually ate, not since her change, but she recognized the scent of it. Her eyelids popped open, and she stared at the ceiling overhead. Watermarked popcorn texture with a sprinkler that had been painted over a few times. She sat up and stared around at the ugly room in consternation.

It looked like a motel last decorated in the eighties or nineties with bold floral patterns and heavy dark wooden furniture with a television so fat it was a wonder the dresser it sat on didn't collapse. The floor was scuffed wooden planks, the varnish long stripped. The walls were made of cheap fake panels no better than cardboard, papered to look like wood. One of her step-daddies had fixed the basement with it. Then put holes in it when he got drunk.

There were no holes here yet but sconces attached to the wall with smoked glass shades. Currently unlit and yet the room was bright enough to see due to the curtains that didn't quite fit the window they were stretched across.

No one else in the room, but she could hear the low murmur of voices. Where were they coming from?

Another sweep of the space showed a door partially ajar. It appeared to be where the bacon smell and voices wafted from. Emma slipped out of bed and noticed she currently wore a tracksuit. Clean and pink.

Who'd dressed her?

She reached for her horn and almost sighed as she found it the same length she recalled. That wasn't always the case. She'd woken up more than once to find it shorn down to a nub. Sphinx claimed they did it to help her. After all, it wasn't as if it hurt.

It didn't, yet she preferred people leave her horn alone. This was the longest it had ever gotten. Shiniest, too. All that liquid iron in its diet.

Ignoring the partially open door that begged exploration, Emma eyed the two other doors in the room. The one with just a plain round knob probably led to the bathroom. The chain on the other was a good indication it led outside. Outside equaled freedom.

She took a few steps in its direction before slowing and stopping. Where would she go? She had no idea where she was. She might emerge somewhere busy. Not exactly something she could do. Going out in public was a normal person activity. Emma was a woman with a horn. People wouldn't stop to talk to her and find out what she was about. Like Oliver, they'd assume she was a monster, and the pitchforks would come out. Or guns. Or cuffs. Didn't really matter what they used to capture her. Blood would be spilled, and she'd be scrubbing her horn furiously, blinking back tears again.

And my horn will shine bright like a diamond. The idea had a giddy appeal she ignored.

Perhaps rather than leave right away, she could find out more about her situation. After all, she wasn't tied down. Whoever took her even took the time to put her in clean clothes.

"I see you're finally awake. Care to join us for breakfast?"

The query startled Emma. She whirled and noticed a face peeked through the doorway, the porcelain skin framed by vivid red tresses. Yet it was the eyes that captivated. They swirled with colors.

Which could only mean— "You're like me," Emma exclaimed.

The ruby-red lips curved into a smile. "Not quite. Those of us given a second chance at life are quite unique. But despite our differences, we do share a common bond, which makes us family."

"You were at the clinic, too?" Emma asked, unable to hide a hint of skepticism. Apart from the strange eyes, the woman appeared beautiful. Contacts would make it easy for her to go out in public.

"I wasn't at the clinic itself, but I received the same

treatment you did. Join us for breakfast and we can fill you in."

"Us? Who is us?"

"More people like you and me. You're safe here, Emma."

Said every predator to draw in their prey. Emma chewed her lower lip. "Who are you? Where am I?"

"I'm Jane. As to where, you're in a safe place."

"Don't bullshit the girl," shouted a gruff voice. "We're only safe until some asshole finds us again and tries to ventilate us."

The woman called Jane rolled her eyes. "Oh, stop being so pessimistic, Jett. The only reason we got caught last time was because someone left her daddy a message telling him where he could join us."

A different female voice replied, "How was I to know he went over to the dark side?"

The friendly arguing was what got Emma's feet moving until she'd crossed the room and peeked through the door into a larger suite equipped with a tiny kitchenette and too many people for the space. Three of the four chairs around the tiny table were filled, and another person sat on the couch with a baby in her lap.

Emma hesitated in the doorway, noticing the fact that they all appeared normal. No horns, tails, or wings. It made her self-conscious.

Jane noticed. "Don't be scared."

"I'm not." A total lie that she hoped the other woman didn't hear. "I don't want to freak them out."

She didn't point to her horn, but Jane flicked a glance to it.

"Oh, please. Do you seriously think any of them care about that? You are among friends, Emma."

So she kept saying. That didn't make it true. "How do you know my name?"

"Because you're the only unicorn in the world. Adrian was so happy to hear you survived the helicopter crash."

"You know Dr. Chimera?"

Those red lips curved into a mischievous smile. "I know him very well actually. And so does everyone in this room."

Emma looked at the other woman. "He fixed everyone here?"

"Most of us," Jane corrected. "Me, Luke, Jayda. Then there's Becky, who worked for him and kind of took the cure on purpose. Only Jett and Margaret are still normies but we're working on changing their minds."

"Not likely. With my luck, I'd end up something stupid like a roach or a dumb llama." Jett, the dark-haired man who'd taken her from the ruins, shook his head.

"You all seem so—" Emma hesitated, not knowing what word to use. Sane? Who was to say those who turned were crazy or just following a natural impulse? They certainly appeared human. Could speak, too. How nice it would be to converse with others who might understand.

People who won't see me as a monster.

"Seem normal? Because we are. Most of the time. We aren't going to try and eat you alive, if that's what you're asking."

"Speak for yourself," the blond guy said with a smirk.

"Luke!" the woman bouncing the baby exclaimed. "Behave yourself. You're scaring her."

Jane smirked. "That's Luke's wife, Margaret. She keeps him in line. Don't worry. If he tries to bite you, she'll smack him. Come on and join us. You have nothing to fear."

Taking a deep breath, Emma crossed the threshold into the other room and once more took in details, from the interested gazes on the faces to the lack of any kind of pity or disgust.

On the contrary, someone exclaimed, "Hot shit, she really is a unicorn."

"Told you so," said smugly.

Looking at the dark skinned woman, unsure if she should be peeved or complimented by the comment, Emma realized she recognized her. "You're Dr. Cerberus's daughter."

"Call me Jayda." The woman raised a hand to salute then nudged the guy beside her. "This lug beside me might seem familiar, too."

"You're Dr. Chimera's guard." It took a wrinkle of her brow to match the name to his granite face. "Jett?"

"Yup."

"Luke," offered the third one sitting at the table, his

hair blond and messy, his eyes a vivid green. "One of the first Chimera screwed around with."

"I thought you went nuts." She slapped a hand over her mouth. "I mean—Sorry—"

Luke laughed. "I did go a little crazy for a bit. But I got my shit together once I met Margaret."

"A good thing, too," said the woman on the couch with a bright smile.

Jane pointed. "In case you didn't figure it out, that's Margaret and their son, Lorcan."

"And you're a group?"

"Kind of," Jayda said. "There're a few others, too. Marcus, my nicer half, is in the other room with Adrian."

"Dr. Chimera?" Emma interrupted.

"Yes, Dr. Chimera is here with us. As are Becky, Jett's wife, and their girls, who are in the bathtub again."

"Only because I told them they couldn't go swimming in the pool yet. Damned thing is green and disgusting." Jett shook his head. "I'm going to hit town today and look for parts to fix the pump."

"You said you have children here. Are they..." Emma glanced at Jane, unsure if she should say anything.

"They're special, too. The only ones who don't have special genes are Jett and Margaret. But you don't have to worry about them. Despite the fact they're mundane, we like them." Jane grinned as Jett huffed, "Mundane my ass."

Introductions were all well and good, but Emma had a more pressing concern. "Why am I here? Actually, how did I get here?"

"We went looking for you. One of the guys who also survived the chopper crash made it out of the mountains. Given one person survived the helicopter crash, Adrian said it might be a good idea to check out the clinic and see if there were more survivors. Are there any others?"

Several pairs of eyes turned to Emma, who realized they waited for an answer. "Yes. Kind of." She sighed. "Depends on your definition of survivor. Seven of us made it out of that chopper."

"Do you remember their names?"

"Yes." Names, faces, the fear she would evolve like they had. She named them. "Xiu. Barry. Jacob. Janice. Felice. Marco. Kelly."

"What of doctors and staff on board?"

"Dead." She ducked her head, her heart pounding as she waited for them to ask how.

They didn't. Rather they wanted to know, "Did you stick together after the crash?"

"Some of them did."

"Were you one of them?"

"Not at first." How to explain she'd wanted to return to the clinic when all they wanted was to escape. In the end, given how a few of them devolved, she didn't regret her decision. When no one said anything, she realized they were waiting for her to elaborate.

"I eventually ran into a few." Drawn by the thought of being with someone. Not alone. "It didn't last long." The madness was already gripping them, and she wanted far, far away lest it infect her, too.

"Have you been living in the clinic this entire time?"

Emma nodded. "Once I found my way back. It took me a few weeks."

"And did you find anyone at the clinic?" asked Jayda.

"You mean other people?" She shook her head.

"What of the thing in the ruins? The oil slick?" Jett asked.

"I don't think you can call him a person anymore," she said sadly. "I think the blob was left behind when they evacuated the clinic. Or it came out of hiding once no one was there to guard it. It already haunted the place when I arrived."

"And it didn't bother you?"

"No." Not much ever bothered her.

"And you never saw anyone else?"

She did, but those appearances were always one-offs. Like that time she caught Kelly watching her bathe from the woods. Next thing she knew, she woke in the forest, face down in a pile of leaves. Her horn in need of another bath.

"Nope. Nobody, except for Oliver." Thinking of him, she wondered where he was. Not that it mattered. He'd betrayed her. Filming her without consent.

Posting the video. Putting her in so much danger because he hated monsters.

He hates me. The reminder made her sad.

"Oh dear. She's looking pale, and here you guys are badgering her. Sit down, Emma. You look famished." Margaret rose from the couch and handed the wiggly child to her husband, who bounced the baby on his knee.

Emma found herself tucked into an empty chair, and a plate of pancakes slid in front of her. Fluffy hot pancakes. And syrup. Not the real kind, but she didn't care. It was sweet and sticky. She devoured it and chugged the glass of orange juice. The first freshly made food she'd had since the evacuation of the clinic.

Only once she pushed the plate away did she realize she'd never actually heard what happened to Oliver.

Don't care.

Just like this group didn't seem to care she had a horn sticking out of her head. If they were to be believed, they were like her. And yet weren't. For one, they weren't raving lunatics. They talked amongst each other, sharing a joking vibe and camaraderie that showed a close bond and intellect.

"Have you been friends a long time?" Emma blurted out.

For some reason, this made Luke laugh. "Fuck no. When we first met, some of us hated each other."

"But..." Emma couldn't help but frown. "If that's the case, how come you're all here together?"

"Common enemy. Common goal. And a discovery that, in spite of our differences, we are the same," Jett replied.

"Not quite, Mundie," teased Luke.

"Don't start, wet dog."

And the banter recommenced. It washed over Emma and warmed her, especially since she didn't feel excluded.

Jane helped Margaret with the dishes while Jett left to check on his family. Only once the last plate was tucked away did Jane fix Emma with her kaleidoscope eyes.

"If you get hungry again, let us know. We have food. Plenty of it."

"Thank you." The idea of fresh meals already made her situation a hundred times better. But she still didn't know what they wanted from her.

"Feel like telling us a few more details about what happened since the crash?"

"Not really," she said with a wan smile. "It's kind of boring and pathetic."

"That would be a refreshing change." Luke's drawled reply.

"How did you survive?" Margaret asked. "I thought the clinic was supposed to be leveled."

"Only the upper layers," Emma said. "The stuff below ground remained mostly intact. So I had access to food and clothing, even my old room and bed."

"I'm surprised more of the survivors didn't follow

your lead." Jayda frowned. "The other escaped projects always returned."

"They returned while Adrian was in residence. Once he moved, they followed." Luke glanced at Emma. "Have you seen any of the others since the winter passed?"

She shook her head.

"So they could be dead," Jayda remarked, drumming her fingers on the table.

"I thought you said someone walked out of the mountains?"

Jane joined them at the table. "Someone did. But the cops got to him before we did. Now we don't know where he is."

"What's his name?"

"John? Jack?" Jayda said, grabbing her phone and tapping on it.

"Jacob?" Emma offered.

"That's it. There's a picture along with some article online. Here." Jayda spun her phone around, and Emma leaned forward to look.

The thin features were easily recognizable. "That's him. He's one of the seven I told you about who walked away."

"Can you tell us what happened? Why did the helicopter crash?"

The question she dreaded finally came. "One of the patients got loose and killed the pilot." Emma didn't tell them which one. Technically she didn't know for sure. The fact no other patient was loose didn't require disclosure.

"You had Sphinx on board?"

"Yes. He's dead."

"Good." Luke didn't hide his pleasure in the news. "Man was a grade-A asshole."

"Did you ever see anyone at the clinic after the crash? I don't mean survivors," Jayda explained. "Any helicopters land or do flybys? Maybe even a drone?"

Emma shrugged. "It took me a few weeks to return. And once winter hit, I didn't go out much." Just daily peeks for fresh air and real light.

"Tell us about the thing in the ruins." They kept asking her questions. Getting her to detail what remained of the clinic, the blob, and the thing in the lake.

The tone of the room turned serious, but she didn't mind because no one threatened. They just wanted to know...everything.

And since Emma had nothing to lose, she answered every question. Unfortunately, her answers weren't very interesting.

Jane tapped her lower lip thoughtfully. "Given we now are aware of seven people who survived the helicopter crash, we might need to go poking around the mountains a bit more."

"Before that, we need to go back to the valley and handle that thing in the lake." Luke's lips pulled taut over sharp teeth. "You up for a hunt, Jayda?"

She pushed off the counter. "I'll see if I can hook us

up with a harpoon before we go. We can't have any of the patients that escaped killing people."

"Surely you're not worried about them getting out of the valley." Emma bounced her gaze between them. "The blob can't stand sunlight, and whatever is in the water is bound by the lake."

"For now. But they might still adapt, or more people might go exploring like that fellow we found you with."

"Oliver?" The reminder meant she couldn't keep pretending he didn't exist. She had to warn them. "You can't trust him. He wants to expose the clinic."

"So we discovered," Jayda said sourly.

"Don't worry about Oliver." Jane's tone was meant to be soothing. "We've got him contained."

"You have him?"

"He's in the other room with Dr. Chimera."

Which immediately drew her gaze.

It took all of her willpower to not approach the door. To toss her head and say casually instead, "What do you want from me?"

"Become a part of our group."

"Doing what?" she asked.

"Figuring out a way we can survive. How to stay out of sight. Finding others and giving them safety too." Jayda's gaze fixed her. "Will you join our cause?"

Asked to be a part of something? To not be an outsider? As if there was any question.

"Tell me what I can do to help."

CHAPTER ELEVEN

Oliver woke but couldn't move. Not a single limb. Eyes wide open, he stared at the unfamiliar water-stained ceiling.

Where am I?

Last thing he recalled he was in the valley, Emma was being put on a helicopter, and some guy with a gun shot him.

But not with a bullet, Oliver realized. Which explained the groggy feeling in his mind and limbs. They'd drugged him. Then kidnapped him.

He was a prisoner. Both wrists and ankles were tied. It brought a thrashing panic to his body that got him nowhere.

When he stopped heaving, a dry voice said, "I wouldn't bother. Jayda is quite good at keeping people restrained."

"Who are you? What am I doing here?" And the one question he didn't ask: *What are you going to do with me?* Because it didn't take much of a leap to realize anyone who had him tied down probably wasn't up to any good.

"My name is Doctor Adrian Chimera, and you are here because you poked your nose in places you shouldn't." A man stepped into view, younger than the images Oliver had managed to dig up. Somewhere in his early thirties rather than the mid-forties he should have been according to birth records. His hair was dark and lush. His body fit and his gaze sharp. No sign of the wheelchair in his high school pictures.

"If it isn't Dr. Frankenstein himself!" Oliver couldn't help the curl of his lip. "What do you want with me? Where's Emma?" Because he recalled her being shot, and despite their differences, he didn't want to see her harmed.

"Emma is fine. As to what I want with you, let's start with some answers." The doctor dragged a chair to the bedside and sat, looking perfectly comfortable in his button shirt, tie, and slacks. The picture of yuppie elegance despite the surroundings and the fact that he questioned a man he kept unlawfully imprisoned.

"I don't have to tell you anything." Probably not the brightest stance to take, yet Oliver wasn't about to spill his guts. Figuratively or literally.

"Are you really going to waste both of our time? You know you're at a disadvantage. You're a smart man, Oliver. I'm sure you see it's best if you cooperate."

Cooperating might get him killed quicker. Best if he stalled. "How do you know my name?"

"Emma told us. Says you know quite a fair bit about the clinic. Which is curious since I've ensured all mention of it—both physical and digital—was wiped. And what I missed, my friend Marcus here"—he gestured to a large man behind him with surfer-blond hair—"found and eradicated. So how did you hear about me and the clinic?"

"None of your business." He strained. "Let me go. You can't keep me here." Wherever here was. They'd probably evacuated him from the valley in a helicopter, and he'd been sleeping who knew how long. They could be anywhere at this point.

"I can and will confine you until I'm satisfied you'll keep your mouth shut."

"That won't ever happen." Again, Oliver's stupidity gene reared itself and he spoke without thought.

"For a smart man, you're being awfully obtuse." Chimera turned to his guard. "Can you leave us alone a moment?"

Marcus didn't even look at Oliver before exiting the room.

The fact that Chimera didn't want the man to see what came next had Oliver bucking. "Fucking bastard. Let me go."

"Calm yourself."

"I will not calm down."

"A shame you don't want to cooperate."

"Why would I cooperate? It's not like I can believe a word that comes from your lips. And given the extremes you've gone to keep your secret, I'm sure your plan is to kill me no matter what." Oliver understood the dire situation.

"Such melodrama. And all based on conjecture. Tell me, Oliver"—Chimera leaned close—"what makes you think you really know me? We've never met."

"I know enough." Cerberus had plenty to say about Adrian Chimera. Some of it glowing. Some of it ripe with jealousy at the younger man with the brilliant mind and ideas.

"How do you know if it's the truth? Or are you one of those people who just relies on one side of the story? Which seems odd given your occupation. Doesn't your bio say you like to get to the truth?"

"You know who I am." Flatly stated.

"It wasn't that hard to find out given we found your notes. That is why you were at the clinic. You're writing a book."

"I'm going to expose what you did. I'm going to make sure the world knows about the monsters so they can get rid of them." Why did he keep saying things he meant to keep quiet? His gaze narrowed on Chimera. "What did you do to me?" Because, he wasn't usually this honest.

"Just a little something I cooked up in the kitchen."

The realization he'd been drugged made Oliver's stomach turn. "A truth serum?"

"Not quite, because truth is subjective, but it does make you a little more likely to speak frankly." Chimera smiled, but it didn't reach his eyes. "So feel free to tell me anything you like. Starting with who gave you the information for your book."

"No one did. I found it." He was happy to see the ability to lie remained.

Chimera didn't buy it for a second. "Since I know there is nothing online to trace back to me, that must mean you spoke to someone. Who was it?"

"None of your business."

"Everything connected to the clinic is my business," Chimera snapped, bursting out of the chair and pacing. "If you spoke to one of my patients, then you need to tell me. I have to help them."

"Haven't you helped them enough?" Oliver muttered.

"Again, so quick to judge my actions based on only one version of events."

Oliver couldn't help but snort. "There are no two sides to this. You experimented on people and made them into monsters."

"Experimented is harsh and does a disservice to my true purpose."

"Let me guess, your true motivation was trying to win the award for evil scientific megalomaniac of the year."

Chimera's lips flattened into a line. "I healed people."

"Not going to deny the evil part?"

"I did what no one else could do."

"Yeah, you created monsters. Way to go." Oliver rolled his eyes to go with the sarcasm.

"A shame you can't see the potential in them. The hope."

"They're not human."

"Perhaps not one hundred percent. But does that really matter? Those I treated, myself included, are still people."

"So you did experiment on yourself, too?"

"I went from crippled in a wheelchair to how you see me now." Chimera posed, the picture of vitality.

"You look normal."

"I should hope so. The goal of the treatment is to make people better, not worse."

"I met the thing in the ruins. A giant blob that sizzles in sunlight and wants to eat flesh. You can't tell me that's better."

"An unfortunate side effect."

Oliver blinked at him in shock before blurting out, "An unfortunate side effect is shitting your pants, not becoming some weird vampire puddle."

"There will be bumps on the road as we aim for success."

"You're a sick fuck." Oliver couldn't help but say it with a curl of his lip. "You don't care about the people you've ruined."

"I care more than the institutions that failed them." Chimera didn't back down. His expression turned angry. "Do you know how many people I saved when hospitals convinced families to pull the plug, in order to free up beds? Those patients were sentenced to die, but because of me, they lived. The man who lost three of his four limbs serving his country? Able to walk again and play sports."

"You make it sound good. But let me guess, that guy who grew his limbs, he's got something wrong with him, doesn't he? Because if this cure was so bloody awesome, you wouldn't be so determined to hide it from the world."

"I hide it because people aren't yet ready to understand."

"You're right. We don't understand because what you're doing is inhumane." Oliver couldn't seem to help himself being angry instead of using the conciliatory tone he'd need to be set free. "If the world found out about you, your patients, the monsters you made..."

"They'd hunt us down and murder us. I know." Said quietly. "Do you think that doesn't prey on me at night? I worry about them all. Despite what you think, I know each of their names."

"But do they remember?" he asked.

Chimera's chin dropped. "Unfortunately, not as many as I'd like. Which is why I must gather them all. Even the broken ones. Who told you about the clinic?"

"I told you, the internet."

"You're lying."

"Hit *YouTube* and you'll see the same newsfeed I did from that doctor dressed like the devil." Oliver mentioned the very public video that was debunked by news sources within hours.

"You did not go exploring in the mountains in that specific spot because of a hoax."

"Except it wasn't a hoax."

"Only a few people actually believe that. I doubt you were one of them. You seem the skeptical sort who needs proof."

"Which I found and already uploaded to the web," Oliver said with a sneer. "You're too late."

"Am I?" Chimera smiled. "We intercepted your transmission. You didn't reveal a thing."

The knowledge burned. "You won't get away with this. Others will come snooping, too."

"Only if the informant keeps talking. But that's not going to happen because you're going to tell us everything you know. Name? If you don't have one, then their appearance."

"I am not going to tell you shit because I know you'll kill anyone who snitches about your secrets."

Chimera offered a cold smile. "You know what they say about loose lips."

"You're a murderer and a monster."

"It's not murder when it's about survival."

"Not going to deny you're a monster?"

The other man arched a brow. "Monster? Or next stage of evolution? It all depends on what lens you choose to view my actions. I prefer the term visionary."

"What you've done is evil."

"It isn't evil to save lives." Chimera defended his actions.

"It is if you're making people into...*things*." Uttered with all the disgust he could manage.

"Such a harsh assessment. I know a few who'd take offense."

"I've seen the results of your experiments."

"I will admit that not all of them turned out quite as I hoped."

"Gee, you mean to say you didn't mean to create a giant octopus?"

"You met Matty?" Adrian asked. "That was unfortunate, what happened to him. Too much, too quick. I learned from that mistake."

"Apparently not, because you kept going, didn't you? Twisting people to your own purpose. Trying to change the face of mankind. You can't be allowed to get away with it. You and your monsters need to be destroyed."

"Even Emma?"

The subtle query had him thinking of her. The delicateness of her features. Her kindness when he'd done nothing to deserve it. She shouldn't be punished.

"A real doctor could probably help her return to a normal life."

Chimera's lips twisted. "The *real* doctors gave her only a few weeks to live. *I* cured her from the disease riddling her body."

"You made her into a freak."

"At least she's not an ass like you." A woman stepped into the room, her skin a shade of brown that glowed with health. Her body very toned in leggings and a form-fitting tank top.

"Lucky me, another of Chimera's ass-kissing syco-phants." Oliver recognized her from the valley.

"For a guy tied to a bed, you're awfully mouthy. And useless, from the sounds of it. Has he told you anything?" She addressed that query to Chimera.

"Oh, he's had plenty to say. Did you know he thinks we're all monsters in need of culling?"

"I'd hate to disappoint him. Let me grab a shovel and I'll bury him in the woods."

Oliver didn't doubt for one minute she'd kill him. "Getting rid of me won't stop your secret from coming out."

"Maybe not, but I'll feel a whole lot better." Said with a not-so-nice smile.

Chimera chided. "Jayda, no taunting our guest. How am I supposed to get him to talk?"

"He's got a pretty face. Let's see how attached he is to it." Jayda rubbed a fist.

"I don't think hitting him is the proper tack to take."

The first thing Chimera said that Oliver agreed with.

"If you need someone to sweet talk him, then throw Margaret at him. She had Emma eating out of her hand in minutes."

"What have you done to Emma?" Oliver demanded. "You'd better not have hurt her."

"Us, hurt her?" Jayda turned an incredulous gaze on him. "You're the one threatening to expose her to the world. Do you know what they'd do to someone rare like her? It's a good thing we found her. Now she can be with people who don't treat her like she's worthless and scary."

"I would have found her help." The words sounded as weak out loud as they did in his head.

The look Jayda cast on him found him wanting. "I'm going to join Marcus on patrol before I twist this guy's head off."

"Any signs of trouble?" Chimera asked.

"No. Just a funny feeling in my gut."

"Should we move?"

She shrugged. "And go where? In one respect, dickhead over there is right. We can't keep hiding forever."

Chimera stroked his chin. "I just need a little more time."

"We ain't got time. Won't be long before people notice there's something strange about us and word gets out."

Strange how? And why did Jayda keep saying we? Was she also one of the Chimera secret patients? Staring at the woman, Oliver didn't see anything abnormal about her. No horns. No glowing eyes. Then again, Chimera himself looked fairly normal. If Cerberus hadn't told Oliver what Chimera had done, would he have known the man was one of the monsters?

Jayda left, and Chimera turned his attention to Oliver again. "Before you ask, she is."

"Is what?"

"One of those monsters you're determined to hate. Which begs the question, who is the real monster? The people who wanted a second chance at life or the man who would see us all eradicated because he fears us?"

"You're changing the face of humanity."

"And?" Chimera queried. "Perhaps you've not noticed, but studies have shown that only species that can adapt as their living conditions change survive."

"Except people aren't adapting naturally. You're changing them with science."

"And you should be thanking me. The world is in dire peril. The climate is shifting. The oceans warming. If you listen to experts, we could face a worldwide cataclysmic event within just a few decades. We're talking about the extinction of humankind if we don't do something."

"If you believe them," he muttered.

"Are you a climate denier, Oliver?" Chimera asked.

Yes and no. He'd written a book that dug into the subject in depth, but he wasn't about to start arguing with the man about it. "You can try and paint what you do any way you like. It's still wrong."

"I see. So you think we should all die and good riddance. Fascinating. And are you the man to do it? Will you be the hand that holds the gun and kills us?" Chimera asked, heading for Oliver's feet and untying them.

The question was a two-edged blade. On the one hand, Oliver did believe in ending the life of monsters before they could multiply and spread their taint. On the other...some of them looked all too human. Like Jayda and Emma.

"Maybe we don't have to kill, but you certainly shouldn't be allowed to roam free." Oliver stuck to his guns.

"Squeamish about culling. What does that leave? Prison?"

"You don't need punishment, but you also can't just wander around freely. Something could be arranged."

Adrian's brows lifted. "Perhaps they'll place us in a zoo where humans can gawk, because putting people in cages for daring to live is so very humane."

"Stop twisting my words."

"How is it twisting? You are the one saying it. The one who believes we shouldn't exist or should be restrained." Chimera reached for Oliver's wrists and untied him.

Freed, Oliver didn't immediately move, mostly because he suspected some kind of trick. "Why are you untying me?"

"Because, contrary to your belief, we are not murderous monsters."

"Why did you kidnap me? Did your crew mess up and think I was one of your secrets?"

"They weren't sure at first, but some bloodwork and the fact I didn't recognize you sorted that part out."

"Why didn't you kill me when you discovered I was out to expose you?" It made no sense. And why did Chimera talk with him? Was it because he planned to dispose of Oliver? In that case, it didn't matter what he revealed. Oliver would take it to the grave.

"I agree killing you would have been easier." Chimera smiled. "It was discussed you know. Once my crew, as you called them, realized you weren't one of us and posed a danger, they recommended extermination. But I talked them out of it once I saw your notes. How old-fashioned of you to pen them rather than type."

"Those were private," Oliver exclaimed hotly.

"As was my clinic and my work. That didn't stop you from digging. Be happy I found and read them. They at least gave you a motive for your actions. You're writing a book about my life's work. Quite flattering I have to say."

"I doubt you'll think so when I'm done." He tried to wrack his brain to see what his notes might have revealed. He'd not brought his notebook that mentioned his interviews with Cerberus. He wondered if those he'd scanned and stored as a PDF in the cloud had been wiped. He hadn't dared check for fear they'd disappear too.

"You seem convinced you know the story. And I am saying you only glimpsed one tiny portion of it. You want to know why you're really here? Because you're a test, Oliver. You're going to spend some time with me, Jayda, Emma, and the others. You're going to meet these people you so easily call monsters. You will talk to them. Eat with them. See them every day."

"To what purpose?"

"Why, to give you fodder for your book. And, who

knows, perhaps by the time you're done with your research, you might realize that the true monsters aren't the ones I cured but the one who is allowing his own jealousy to put everyone at risk. You listened to Dr. Cerberus and his one-sided tale. Now, don't you think it's fair I get a turn?"

"Who?"

"Don't play stupid. I know exactly who spoke to you. It's in your damned notes."

"I never said a name."

Chimera sneered. "You didn't have to. Only one other person could have known and told you about some of the things you referenced. And let me just say, Cerberus is far guiltier in some respects than I ever was. At least I could claim I did it to help people."

With those words, Chimera turned and left through a door that spilled sunshine into the room for a moment before it shut. Oliver didn't hear the sound of a lock, nor did anyone return to tie him up again.

Could it be true? Was he truly free to get up and move around? Investigate and talk to the very people who'd taken him prisoner? A suspicious nature meant he sought an ulterior motive.

He said he wanted me to spend time with the people here. Implying there were more than a few. A whole bunch of monsters in one place. Surely the man jested. It seemed like a recipe for a horror movie.

With me as the guy getting murdered and eaten. Only if he lay around and allowed it. *Get your ass moving.*

Oliver rolled out of the bed and stumbled, his limbs a little stiffer than expected. How long had he been knocked out? He didn't ask and had no way of telling. He glanced around the ugly motel room. The kind that Norman Bates and his mother would have loved.

On spaghetti legs, Oliver made it to the door, placed his hand on the knob, and hesitated. What if this were a trick? Perhaps the plan was to make him think he could open that door and just walk away. Surely if he tried someone would stop him.

But what other choice did he have? There was only one other door in the room, gaping wide on a bathroom patterned with ancient beige and brown tile. A quick peek inside showed a window too small to squeeze his ass through.

The choice boiled down to sit around like a victim or walk out the front door. With his heart pounding harder than the time he smuggled a USB stick with stolen information from a dictator-controlled country, he yanked open the door and blinked at the bright daylight outside.

Nobody screamed a warning. Shots weren't fired. He stood unnoticed in the warm sunshine. He'd guessed correctly about this being a motel. The room he emerged from boasted a blue door, the paint peeling and faded in places. It matched the other doors running the stretch of the long building, each one in a different primary color—yellow, green, blue, and red. A few doors had plastic chairs—the woven kind that gave unsuspecting bare legs and butts waffle skin— sitting outside them on the concrete walkway.

The parking lot appeared rather empty with only two vehicles in it. One was a large suburban with tinted windows. The other a navy blue sedan.

Hearing laughter, Oliver glanced to his left and noticed a few picnic tables sitting on scraggly, long grass bordered by a thin line of trees, just enough to screen from the road that went past. Not a very busy road given he'd yet to see a car. Just past the table he noted a chain link fence and a shimmer of water indicating a pool.

There were people milling around, such as the man tossing a squealing child in the air while a woman watched them. Another fellow stood by the pool's edge, holding a towel in his hands with another one draped over his shoulder. A steady *creak, creak* drew Oliver's attention to a swing set, the chains swaying back and forth making the noise. Sitting on the plank, pumping her legs was someone with a familiar face— and horn.

Emma! Elation filled him, along with relief. Which struck him as strange. He barely knew the woman, not to mention she was technically still a monster. So why would he worry about her well-being? Probably another effect of the drug.

He should be more concerned with how he could escape and gather proof to bring with him. Obviously, this many mutants in one spot could only spell trouble. Maybe even a coup. Was Oliver present at ground zero? Could he stop it from spreading?

His gaze roved again, taking in details, realizing that to speak might condemn the lady with the baby to incarceration, possibly death. Everyone he looked at appeared so damned human.

Even Emma, who still pumped her legs and laughed when she reached the apex of her swing.

Oliver didn't realize he still stared at Emma until her gaze met his and he saw the smile on her lips fade. She intentionally turned her face from him.

Shunned him.

His happiness at seeing her deflated. Anger rose in its place. Anger that she rejected him? Surely not. Probably it stemmed more from the fact he'd been taken prisoner and interrogated while she played on the swing, not worried about him at all.

Which probably wasn't fair to her. After all, what could she do?

She could have checked on me. Then again, why would she? At their last confrontation he'd essentially ignored her wishes and attempted to broadcast her existence to the world. Would she ever understand he'd done it to help? Perhaps once her secret got out, she could get real treatment, starting with the removal of the thing that made her different. Once she fit in with everyone else, she'd thank him.

Or was that wishful thinking?

Funny how as she hopped off the swing it wasn't her glittering horn that drew the eye but the shape of her. Womanly in her jeans and a snug Henley shirt. Her hair spilled over her shoulders in a silken wave that dangled down her spine. He got a nice view of her swaying backside as she walked away.

For some reason the fact that she shunned bothered him. "Emma?" He called out her name, and he thought for a moment she would continue to ignore him. However, her shoulders squared, and she pivoted on her heel to walk in his direction.

She didn't wear a smile, though. "You finally woke up," she stated when she got close enough.

"No thanks to your friends and their drugs. How long was I out?"

"A while. And you're lucky to be alive. They dosed you with some powerful stuff."

"Strong enough to take down monsters." The comment slipped past his lips, and he regretted the words, even as he couldn't stop them.

"What is wrong with you?" She recoiled, and he felt like a heel, but that didn't stop him from doubling down.

"Wrong with *me*? Are you really going to go there? Is that why you stole my phone in the first place? So you could call up your monster buddies to come get you?" he accused.

Her gaze turned frosty. "They came looking for me because they heard there were survivors from the helicopter crash."

"Yeehaw, they found you. In case you didn't notice, they also kidnapped me."

"I'm sure they regret it." She crossed her arms, her expression clearly saying she regretted it, too.

It didn't help the irritation simmering inside. "They're going to kill me."

"Oh, gee, kind of like what you planned for them?" The arched brow showed no sympathy.

Probably because he was being a selfish ass. "Aren't you suspicious at all about their intentions? What do they want from you?"

"To keep me safe."

"And you believe them?" he barked, more harshly than he should have.

It only served to angle her chin higher. "As a matter of fact, I do. And before you say it, yes, I might be wrong. Probably am given my history with trusting people. I mean, after all, I trusted you. And what a mistake that turned out to be."

The barb stung. "I never hurt you. The video never made it online."

"Only because you didn't get the chance. You've made it clear you hate me."

"I don't hate you." The truth.

She clearly didn't believe it. "Liar. I know you hate what I am."

There was no denying that part. "What happened to you is not your fault."

"How condescending of you to say that," she replied with heavy sarcasm.

"I was going to get you some help."

"What if I don't want your kind of help? Did it ever occur to you that I'm happy how I am?"

He gave her an incredulous look. "How can you be happy? You have a horn sticking out of your head."

"And? I think it's pretty."

Glinting in the sun as it did, held majestically aloft, he actually couldn't disagree. "You let that doctor convince you to keep it."

"He didn't have to. Dr. Chimera accepts me for who I am. Everyone here does. The only person who thinks I should change is you."

He flattened his lips. "I'm not the bad guy here."

"Actually, you are because you would see me and everyone else connected to the Chimaeram Clinic locked up or worse."

"Don't talk to me about being locked up. Your precious doctor kidnapped me and is keeping me prisoner here."

"Doesn't it suck to be you," she muttered. "I mean look at the cage he's put you in. The chains you have to wear. The awful gowns and gruel and the endless needles... Hold on, I'm thinking more of what humans would do if they got their hands on me. Oops. My bad."

His turn to grit his teeth. "Why must you be so..."

"So what, Oliver? Feisty? Am I not being docile enough? Would you like me to be the monster you keep accusing me of being? Sorry. Can't help you there. I'm a vegetarian, which means your flesh is safe from me. But I can't guarantee Luke won't eat you."

She jerked her head in the direction of the man approaching them.

"Is this asshole bugging you, Ems?" asked the fellow, his hair waving into wild tufts that should have looked stupid but gave him a rugged air.

"Oliver is just a bit grumpy because of his long nap."

"Lucky bastard. I haven't had a straight three hours' sleep since the kid was born." Said with exasperation at odds with the fond expression he shot toward the child cradled in a woman's arms.

"You are?" Oliver asked at a loss. Cerberus had mentioned names but, unfortunately, didn't have any pictures to go with them.

"Luke." The man held out his hand, and Oliver hesitated a moment before shaking it. Almost wincing at the tight grip.

"Oliver."

"I know. You're some kind of writer, I hear. Got a couple of books published."

"A few." Best not to go into too much detail, given his most famous stuff involved the exposing of scandals.

"Hear you're planning to write about Adrian and the clinic."

Oliver wanted to lie because he saw the dangerous glint in Luke's eyes, but fibbing would probably be worse. "I am. Thinking of calling it *Chimera's Secrets*."

Laughter barked out of Luke. "Oh, he'll like that. Named after him. Then again, that would be apt."

"Are you one of his employees or patients?" Because Oliver couldn't quite tell. The man appeared one hundred percent human, from his healthy mien to his fit body.

"Ex-patient. I'm all cured now." Luke thumped his chest. "Stronger than before even."

"What about the side effects?"

The teeth in the wide smile appeared larger than necessary. "What about the side effects?"

Oliver didn't recoil. "Do you have any?"

"Why should I tell you anything?"

Despite the situation, Oliver couldn't help his curiosity and fascination. "Chimera told me to mingle and get your stories."

"Ah, yes. Adrian and his stupid plan. He has this warped idea that he can change your mind about us. I think he's full of shit, which is why I'm gonna be watching you like a wolf. And if you make one wrong step—"

"Chomp!"

The sudden snap of teeth from behind made Oliver jump, and he whirled to see a huge man with long blond hair had managed to sneak up on him.

"Who the fuck are you?" he managed to exclaim.

"Name is Marcus." The big guy held out his hand and didn't try to crush Oliver's when he shook it. "Also an ex-patient of Adrian's."

"Another one?"

"Yup. When you write the book, you might want to mention that, because of Dr. Chimera, I went from being a guy who was a giant nerd who couldn't get laid to the luckiest fellow alive with the hottest girlfriend ever."

"No need to flatter me. You were already getting laid later," Jayda shouted on her way to the motel.

"I have a hard time seeing you as a virgin," Oliver muttered. He stared at the guy who looked like he could grace a fitness magazine cover.

"That's 'cause you didn't know me before the change when I was a hundred and fifty pounds soaking wet with the thickest glasses you ever saw."

Oliver eyed the guy up and down. "Jeezus," he breathed. The transformation, if true, was startling, but that didn't make it right.

"Please, don't inflate his head any more than it is. Marcus is already insufferable," Luke goaded. "Thinks because he's part lion that he's better than me."

"Lion?" Eying Marcus, Oliver could see it. "What does that make you then?"

Luke puffed out his chest. "Wolfman. Awoooo." He gave a little howl, which was echoed by his child. It sent a chill down Oliver's back. Especially since he made the connection.

"Your kid is a monster, too?"

Oliver hit the ground hard, landing on his ass. He blinked as the delayed reaction to pain hit. "What the fuck?" he exclaimed. He'd never even seen the fist coming

Luke leaned down, the expression in his eyes flinty. "Call my boy a monster again, and they'll never find your body." The guy strutted off, and Marcus shook his head as he stared down at Oliver.

"You were lucky Luke's in a good mood and Margaret is watching. If Jett would have heard you talking smack about his girls, you'd be dead."

"Let me guess. Jett is another of Chimera's patients," Oliver grumbled, getting to his feet.

"Actually, Jett's as human as Margaret. But his wife ain't. And neither are his girls, so you might want to watch your mouth around them."

The blond fellow sauntered off, and Emma, who'd remained silent during the exchange, gave him a look that made him shrink inside.

"Has it ever occurred to you that maybe you should judge people on their merits and not the DNA they carry?" she chided.

Then she left him, too, and Oliver could only watch—miserably—as everyone had fun but him because, in their eyes, he was the one with the problem.

CHAPTER TWELVE

"I NEED YOU TO TRY AND BE NICE TO OLIVER," DR. Chimera—who'd insisted she call him Adrian—said when she stomped into the main motel room, muttering about stupid men.

A scowl pulled at her features. "I was trying to, but he just can't help being an ass. He thinks we're all monsters."

"He is partially right."

Her mouth snapped shut at the betrayal. "How can you agree with him? I thought we were all special. A part of something grand and life changing."

"We are. All of us, beautiful and unique and dangerous. Which is why we cannot pretend and lie about the fact that we are different. Keep in mind I'm not just talking about biological or physical changes. In here." Adrian tapped his temple. "The way we think, act, and feel have also shifted."

"I still feel like me," she insisted.

"Of course you do. However, that doesn't mean that you *are* the same. When I first met you, you were shy and beaten down. The Emma we rescued from that alley never met my gaze. You kept your head ducked, your words emerged soft, and you had difficulty using the word no."

"Because I used to be scared."

"And now you're not. Why?"

She frowned. "Because I know you won't hurt me." At least, so far as she knew, Adrian hadn't. "And I can protect myself from people who do." Sphinx had learned that lesson too late.

"Speaking of protect, you didn't hurt Oliver."

"I almost did at the ruins. Your people stopped me."

"Yet before he pushed you over that edge, you held back, even though he scared you."

"No, he doesn't." Which was only a partial truth. She didn't fear him per se, but what he might represent terrified her.

Adrian shook his head. "Don't lie. I know you are scared. The man threatened to expose you. He wanted to see you captured. Locked away."

"Just because he wanted it didn't mean it was happening."

"Because you acted. You said no." Adrian smiled triumphantly. "Old Emma would have taken what he dished as her due. New Emma doesn't let people walk all over her anymore. New Emma stands up for herself."

"If I'm so self-centered now, then why didn't I let him die? It would have been better for me if he had." Yet even now, she knew she couldn't do it.

"Compassion is not a failing, Emma. You didn't let fear or anger control you. You acted and did what you felt was right."

"But was it right?" She still wondered if she'd made the right choice.

"Everything happens for a reason."

Her nose wrinkled. "Since when do you ascribe to a Zen-like philosophy?"

Adrian shrugged. "A lot of things have been coming clear of late. We are entering a phase in our lives where our choices will decide our future."

"Choices like letting a guy live, even though he's determined to convince the world monsters should be erased?"

"A man who might surprise us yet."

"Doubtful. Oliver hates us."

"Now who's passing judgment?"

She sighed. "I don't know how you think keeping him around will change his mind." He didn't see her as a woman or even a person.

"Well, it certainly won't happen with that attitude. If you expect him to give us a chance, then we need to give him one, too."

"And what if we just reinforce his belief?"

Adrian's face hardened. "Then we do what we must to keep ourselves safe."

Emma knew what that meant.

Kill Oliver and bury him deep enough no one would ever find the body.

The thought brought a sad pang. But how else to avoid his death? Adrian seemed to believe they could change his feelings, and in that moment, she believed it was never going happen.

A theory she revisited when, over the next few days, Oliver not once tried to escape. He went into silent observation mode, sitting outside of the motel, pad of paper in his lap, a sentinel keeping watch as they got fresh air.

He scribbled again at night, listening as they discussed their plight and researched some of the news and social media tidbits Marcus dug up online.

Apparently, before they took over the dilapidated motel, they were living in the tropics until Jayda got a hold of her dad, Dr. Cerberus. The man had been kidnapped months ago from the clinic and finally resurfaced. But he'd changed.

According to Adrian, Dr. Cerberus had gotten it in his head that he'd been maligned at the clinic. That he, not Dr. Chimera, should have the majority of the glory.

Could also be the treatment speaking. Adrian had shown Emma the television appearance that clearly showed the horns on Cerberus's head. The mad glow in his eyes.

He looks like someone who's given in to the dancing spots. He presented a prime example of what happened when the darker half of the cure won. Apparently, that was who Oliver had gotten his initial information from. The devil was the one who'd shaped his beliefs. It explained a lot about Oliver's attitude.

What it didn't explain was her fascination with him. She couldn't help but stalk him. She kept a subtle eye on his every move, convinced he would betray them. Surprised when he didn't. Certain it was just a matter of time.

He's gathering evidence before blowing the whistle.

Over those first few days at the motel, Oliver got to meet the more successful stories that came out of the Chimaeram Clinic. Spying on him meant she saw him watching everything. What they ate, how they laughed, and, in the case of Margaret, even cried—because Luke went into town and brought her back a present for her birthday.

He spoke to some of them, his expression curious, even intent at times. His hand moved furiously as he wrote. But he didn't approach Emma.

By day three, everyone had settled into a cautious routine. Oliver had now become a mainstay, which meant there was a bit of a more relaxed attitude around him. Lorcan, Luke's son, took advantage of it.

His mother had set him down on the ground to toddle while she hung some clothes on a clothesline they'd strung up. The child, with stiff legs and wide-spread arms, headed toward Oliver, who sat in one of the chairs outside the rooms writing.

Emma happened to be close by—big surprise—and saw a worried Margaret move toward her child, only to have Adrian stop her.

They all watched to see what Oliver would do next. The baby—whose motor skills exceeded that of a normal six-month-old—not only managed to grab hold of the chair to climb it he perched in Oliver's lap, snared his pen, and happily slobbered all over it. When Lorcan got bored of that—ten seconds later—he jabbed it at the paper. Probably ruined Oliver's morning notes.

Emma held her breath. Especially since she remembered a similar incident when she was little. It involved her getting thrown to the floor and her bottom paddled by a man who didn't stick around long enough to be called daddy.

Oliver smiled and said something soft to the baby, who chortled.

Everyone uttered a sigh of relief. That evening at dinner, Oliver didn't bat an eye when Lorcan decided to eat off his plate—although he didn't eat much from it after the baby spat out a mouthful of veggies in favor of the meat.

The following day, Oliver was sitting by the pool when Becky emerged from the motel with the twins. Less than a month old and petite, they snuggled in their mother's arms, quiet and well behaved.

Until they saw the water. Then they wiggled and jiggled, their cries sharp and happy. Becky couldn't toss them in the pool fast enough.

Which seemed horrifying the first time you saw it. After all, these were infants!

But they were also part mermaid. The twins dove into the water like pros, sluicing it and bouncing out of it, spitting the liquid at each other. They could breathe as easily in the water as out. While the girls hadn't grown fins, their webbed fingers and toes helped them move through the water. Their skin, the only thing about them that changed when they got wet, shimmered, the fine scales iridescent and beautiful.

That day, under Jett's watchful eye—and gun— Oliver put aside his pen and paper and stripped down to his boxers. He slid into the water, gasping, "It's cold." But he didn't get out. He stood in the shallow end, shivering and waiting.

It didn't take long before one of the twins came over to show off. Arrowing underwater for him then leaping from it at the last minute, twisting to land with a splash.

Emma stifled a giggle as Oliver's face got soaked.

Jett didn't feel a need to constrain himself. "That's my girls."

Once more, Oliver didn't act as expected when confronted with the evidence of the side effects of Chimera's treatment. Instead he was smiling and splashing along with the babies, doing his best to keep his gaze away from Becky, who hovered underwater in the deep end, a deadly siren who would act at any sign of a threat.

By the time their playtime was done, the baby girls were snuggling up to Oliver, who handed them out one by one to Jett, who wrapped them in a towel. No words were exchanged, but something passed between the men, a gaze of understanding, acknowledgement.

Could Adrian be right? Was convincing people as simple as reminding them that the so-called monsters were still human at heart?

Maybe the others were, but with Emma, there was no escaping the very visible horn on her head. Which was the excuse she used to avoid going near Oliver but not the real reason she wouldn't talk to him.

There was something about Oliver that confused. For one thing, she was still attracted to him despite all he'd done, the things he'd said. He drew her. Made her feel a warm tingle between the legs.

A tingle she wouldn't act on. She knew what happened when she let her libido do her thinking. It always started out okay. After a while, the name-calling started then the hitting.

But that was the old me. New Emma didn't take abuse. She dished it.

The fact that she could handle herself meant she got put into the guard rotation. The motel belonged to Adrian, more or less, through several layers of shell companies. It meant they didn't have to worry about other guests. Human guests. And they had a place to bring patients when they found them. Not that they found many alive.

Jayda and Luke were usually the pair sent out on retrieval, with Jett joining them on some occasions. At other times he alternated with Marcus, who usually provided tech support.

Most leads they followed ended up as dead ends. Literally. The ex-patients too far-gone and necessitating elimination. But they did manage a few rescues. Xiu, who'd been placed in an asylum for the blind and predicted her rescue so well, was standing by the exit door holding a bag filled with clothes.

They even found Jacob, that coward who'd left those who crashed with him in the helicopter behind in order to save himself. Apparently, being in human custody hadn't changed him much. He was still an asshole, and the first thing he advocated for upon arriving was Oliver's death.

"Let me take him somewhere. He's a danger to the cause," Jacob claimed.

"If he becomes a liability, we'll handle it," Adrian countered.

That should have been the end of it, but Emma saw the way Jacob watched Oliver. She didn't trust Jacob one bit. Which was weird because she had more in common with him than Oliver.

However, Oliver wasn't the same man she'd met in the ruins. On his fourth day at the motel, she mustered up the courage to approach him.

He was scribbling like a madman at one of the picnic tables. Adrian had given him notebooks, claiming if he was going to write a book he'd need to take lots of notes. No one yet trusted him near a computer.

"Hey, Ollie." She'd adopted the nickname the others used.

He lifted his head, and she noticed the wariness in his gaze but also the pleasure. "Hey."

She wondered if he'd ask why she'd been avoiding him. What would she say?

"It's nice to see you," he said instead.

She searched for a hint of mockery and found only sincerity in his gaze.

"Whatcha writing about today?" she asked, taking a seat beside him.

"Marcus's story."

"Really?" she said, interest piqued. "Did he tell you how he was barely coherent for a while but then got his mind back?"

"Yeah. He even showed me his file from after the accident. He almost died."

"Yup. You'll notice that's a trend with all of Adrian's patients. Like me."

"But you actually agreed to receive his treatment. Not all of them could give consent." Oliver remained caught on that salient point.

"You're right; some couldn't. But let me ask you, if you were in a coma and dying, what would you want doctors to do?"

He put down his pen and laid it across the notebook in his lap. "Honestly? I don't know. I mean, before learning about Chimera and all his secret remedies, I would have said pull the plug."

"But?" she prodded.

"He actually found a way to pull the dying back from the edge. To give those who were missing limbs their legs and arms back. He cured Becky's lung cancer. Breast cancer and more in you. His actions have kept people from dying."

"They have."

"But all of his cures have a price."

"I guess the question is, how high is too high?" she asked. "For me, I get a lovely horn." She raised her hand to it, intentionally drawing his attention.

"And Becky can swim like a fish, as can her twin daughters." He glanced at the pool, where, once more, Jett kept watch while his girls frolicked.

"Are mermaids monsters?" she asked softly.

It took him a while to answer. "If I say no, then I have to ask myself why. Why would they be considered okay compared to a werewolf?"

"Luke prefers the term wolfman since he doesn't actually become a wolf," she said with a soft laugh.

"So he reminded me during our conversation. You know what else he told me? That he's not bothered by it. Not now at any rate. I talked to him you know. Apologized for what I said about his kid, and he confessed something to me." Oliver looked at her.

"What?"

"That there'd been a time he thought he was a monster. That he believed he should die. Do you know what changed his mind?"

"Margaret." Love saved the beast.

Oliver nodded. "Having someone who saw him for who he was and not what he'd become."

"Now that you've talked to him, you're seeing him as a person, too, aren't you?"

Again, he paused before answering. "When I was

inside the clinic, it was easy to condemn the monsters as all evil. I mean that leeching black puddle and the tentacle thing in the lake, they only reinforced my ideas. But then..."

"You met real people."

"I did. And now..." He sighed and raked a hand through his hair. "Now I have to re-evaluate everything I thought. I also need to apologize to you."

"Me? For what?"

"For being an asshole. For calling you a monster. You never asked to be different. You just wanted what we all do, a chance to live."

"In your defense, it can't be easy to meet a woman with a horn on her head." She couldn't afford to melt at his words, so she reminded him, and herself, of the distance between them.

"Don't let me off the hook. I was a dick to you, yet you never did anything but help me. You saved me." He met her gaze, an intense look that did something to her insides, brought a fluttery feeling to her heart. "Thank you."

"You're welcome." She ducked her head.

"I don't suppose I can ask you more about your experience."

"Go ahead."

Somewhat bemused, she began talking, answering questions about the treatment itself. Did it hurt? Was she awake during it? How did she feel when the horn appeared?

"The first time I saw it in a mirror, I cried." The

sight of the knob on her forehead made her feel like she was still being punished.

"Punished for what?" Oliver asked.

"Not lying down and dying like nature intended."

"And now? What do you think?"

Her lips curved into a soft smile. "Now, I see it as a reminder that I was special enough to be given a second chance."

"Did she tell you it's also a deadly weapon?" Jacob arrived with a swagger, his expression smug. Or so it seemed. Her view of him would probably remain forever tainted by his selfishness after the crash.

"Have you harmed someone with it?" Oliver had a tiny crinkle between his eyes.

She wanted to gore Jacob for having taken their moment of understanding and ruining it.

"I've protected myself," she said, not meeting Oliver's gaze.

"Ha. I saw what you did to the doctor on the helicopter. Ventilated him right good." Jacob guffawed.

Blood boiling, she blinked as spots danced in front of her eyes. "Dr. Sphinx wasn't a nice doctor."

"Then I'm sure he deserved whatever he got," Oliver said, getting to his feet and taking her side. "Good thing she saved your ass."

Jacob bristled. "I would have done something if I wasn't all tied up."

"Really? I doubt that. I remember how you acted after the crash," she snapped.

"Nothing wrong with looking after oneself."

"Nope, nothing wrong with being selfish at all." She rose and stepped away from the picnic table. "I gotta go." Somewhere she could calm down before the rage took over and she woke up with her horn a little longer—and covered in blood

CHAPTER THIRTEEN

Emma left Oliver with Jacob, whose sly face would look better with a fist in it.

"She's a nice piece of ass," Jacob declared, watching her leave.

"You shouldn't talk about her like that. She's been through a lot."

"That's priceless coming from you. I'm on to you, *Ollie.*"

"What's that supposed to mean?"

"Those idiots"—Jacob jerked his head in the direction of the motel—"think they can change your mind about us. But we both know that's bullshit. You still want to see us dead, don't you, Ollie?"

"The murderous examples, yes. The monsters I saw in the clinic are too dangerous. But the people I've met here...they deserve a chance."

"Pretty words. Pity I don't believe it. You're playing

us. Trying to get us to trust you when we both know the first stab at freedom you get, you'll turn on them."

"You have no idea what you're talking about."

Jacob sneered. "I know your kind. Which is why I'm going to give you a warning. Leave. Now. Because if you don't..." The words trailed off ominously.

But Oliver wasn't about to be intimidated by this asshole. "Or what? You'll kill me? You don't have the balls."

"Who says it will be me? All it would take is one accusation. A hint in the right ear about the fact you're planning to double cross us and they'll eliminate you for me."

"The people here aren't stupid. They aren't going to blindly swallow your lies." Or would they? Jacob was one of them.

"You keep telling yourself that." Jacob left with a sneer.

Which meant Oliver got to deal with doubt.

Would they kill him if they thought he wasn't on their side? He knew Adrian Chimera kept him around in the hopes of changing his thoughts about the treatment and patients. And it worked.

It was hard to keep the mindset of killing the monsters when a child with a gap-toothed grin snuggled in his lap. How could he condone the murder or even imprisonment of the twins, who were fairy tale creatures come to life and adorable to boot?

Even the adults won him over, and not only with their words and actions. He could see the caring in them for each other. The love. The acceptance without judgment in spite of the fact they were all different.

The world with all its divisions could learn a lot from them.

And Oliver could be the one to spread the word. Problem was he'd gone from wanting to expose the Chimera Secrets to coming around to understanding them, realizing he could never tell anyone.

To tell about even one would be to put them all in danger.

He couldn't be responsible for that, which was why Emma found him that evening burning his notes on a barbecue by the picnic table.

"What are you doing?" she exclaimed.

"Burning my book."

"What?" She gaped at him then at the crinkling edges of paper as he fed them, sheet by sheet, into the fire.

"I can't publish it."

"Because you still think we're monsters." Her statement held a hint of sadness.

He was quick to correct. "On the contrary, it's because you're not that I can't ever let these words see the light of day. You're right about the world not being ready for you yet."

"But if you changed your mind, then surely—"

The shake of his head was more violent than he'd meant. "That's just it. I did come to realize my belief was wrong, but only because I spent time with you. Those who will judge and hate, like I once did, won't get that same opportunity. They'll see the pictures and make assumptions."

"Meaning I'll never have a normal life." Her lips turned down.

He didn't lie. "No. Not a public one at any rate, but here, surrounded by those who understand and accept..." He swept a hand. "You can live outside of a cell or a cage."

"Doomed to be alone. Because, in case you hadn't noticed, everyone here is already hooked up, and I don't think any of them are into sharing." Her smile was lopsided.

"Not everyone. There is Xiu and Jacob." The very mention of that man's name brought a sour taste to his mouth.

"Ugh. Jacob." She wrinkled her nose. "No thanks. I'd rather be alone."

He couldn't help but chuckle. "I'm sure others will come." Words he choked out because, looking at her by the light of the fire, he couldn't help but wish circumstances were different. There was something special about Emma, and it had nothing to do with her horn.

Her soft-spoken manner. Her caring nature. The way she had of ducking when shy and, at the same time, her boldness. Her laughter had the ability to warm him. Her smile squeezed something inside.

Holy shit, I'm falling for her. A week ago, he would have said impossible. Yet the more time he spent with her, with all of the Chimera people, the more he found himself comfortable and even feeling for their plight.

How difficult to live always looking over a shoulder. Wondering if the car that pulled into the lot might bring trouble. If a phone call might be traced.

It also made relationships complicated. For those who were single at any rate. Oliver couldn't blame Emma for not being interested in Jacob. The guy was a dick. But even if he wasn't, Oliver wouldn't want them hooking up. He was old enough to recognize the jealousy at the idea of Emma being with someone else.

Thing was he wasn't sure they should get together either. He liked her, and he no longer feared some kind of viral mutation if they were in close contact. But there was more than just sex to worry about. How would they live as a couple? It wasn't as if he could take her to the movies or out to dinner. Living with her in the open could never happen. Could he truly stay at this hotel, or some other protected place, for the rest of his life just to be with her?

What of his family? His mother would look for him. Knowing her, she wouldn't give up until he was found.

Then there was Cerberus, still a prisoner at the pharmaceutical lab. Without Oliver's exposé, would that company go ahead mass producing a cure they couldn't predict or control? Even Adrian Chimera himself admitted there were more failures than successes. Sure, the treatment was worth using on those who had no hope because at least they had a chance. But he doubted the pharmaceutical company would stop at healing only the direst cases.

Society couldn't handle too many of the lake octopus or the vampire blob. Hell, look at Cerberus himself, a man who not only looked like the devil but began talking like one, too. He still remembered the man's last words: *"The end of times is coming, Oliver. And I shall be the one to lead the legion that rises."*

Someone should stop him. Which was why that evening Oliver knocked on Adrian Chimera's door.

The man answered, shirtless and flushed, which might have had to do with the heat pouring out of his room. "Is something wrong, Oliver?"

"Can we talk?"

"I assume it's important."

At Oliver's nod, Adrian pulled the door wide and beckoned him inside. Upon entering, Oliver noted Jane sat on a chair, looking prim in a robe and, at the same time, sassy with her smirk.

"I'm sorry, I didn't mean to disturb you," he stuttered, cluing in to why Adrian looked unkempt.

"It's fine. Jane and I were just talking."

The claim made Jane snicker.

Oliver had spoken with her recently. Her story was one of the more tragic ones, given she was asleep for two decades before the cure worked. But she was also one of the grandest successes—and secretive ones. He'd yet to find out what side effect she, and Adrian for that matter, suffered. She appeared perfect if you ignored her swirling, multi-colored eyes.

"You look so serious, Ollie," Jane stated, fixing him with her strange gaze.

"We need to talk about Cerberus."

"What about him??" Adrian asked, taking a seat on the couch. Jane joined him, leaving Oliver to stand or take the seat she'd vacated.

He chose to pace. "Remember how you asked me how I knew about you and the clinic?" He didn't wait for a reply. "I had an informant. Someone close to you."

"I thought we already ascertained you'd spoken to Cerberus."

"I did. But when you asked me where he was, I lied." Oliver had told them Cerberus disappeared.

Adrian exploded off the couch. "You know where he is and are only now telling me? You know he's dangerous."

"Yeah, I know." Oliver scrubbed a hand through his hair. "He's not running around if that's what you're worried about. It's actually worse than that. Last time I saw him wasn't at that bar like I told you. He is being held by Leyghas Labs."

"What do you mean, held? Explain." Adrian folded his arms and glared.

"According to his story, Cerberus was approached by Leyghas Labs after that news conference of his. A recruiting team of lawyers drew him in by saying they wanted to hire him. Offered him a huge contract if he'd drop out of sight and work with them exclusively."

"But?" Adrian asked more quietly.

"Leyghas isn't exactly an up-and-up kind of place. The owner is cutthroat. When Cerberus arrived for the meeting to sign the papers, he was sedated and placed in a secure location inside one of their labs."

"That was dumb," Adrian declared. "Cerberus is dangerous."

"So they learned. Apparently, they weren't the first human outfit to try and use him."

"He massacred the first group and escaped," Adrian confirmed. "Which is why I'm surprised this lab managed to contain him."

"Apparently, Cerberus had difficulties blending in with the public. Hence why he tried to come out. When that backfired, he took the offer of a safe place to hide. Once they got him where they wanted him, he couldn't escape."

"What was your role in this? How did you meet him and find all this out?"

Oliver squirmed under the scrutiny. "The owner of the lab knows me and requested me to write a book about the Chimaeram Clinic."

"How is a book condemning the cure supposed to benefit them?"

"Because it wasn't supposed to be a book on the negative aspects. They wanted me to promote the good. The fact it could cure just about anything. They wanted me to make them seem like the saviors of the medical world. But after meeting Cerberus, and hearing him..." Oliver paused and looked at his feet, unable to look Adrian in the eye. "I couldn't do it. "

"And now?"

Oliver sighed. "I still can't do it, but not for the

reason you might think. It has become clear that the treatment can do a lot of good."

"But it can also be bad. It's not something that should be mass manufactured and administered willy-nilly. On that we agree."

"Question is, what will we do about Cerberus?" It was Jane who asked the most important question.

"The good news is Cerberus only knows part of the technique used to create the various serums." Adrian offered a tight smile. "Many scientists are paranoid about having their work stolen, so we tend to keep something back. While he knows most the mechanics, he doesn't have the know-how to actually create the serum."

"Which is probably why Leyghas was acquiring all the ex-Chimera patients it could find."

"They're trying to reverse-engineer the cure," Adrian muttered, taking over from Oliver when it came to pacing. "Which will fail."

"And when they realize they can't recreate it, they'll come after you again," Jane remarked. She fixed her strange gaze on Adrian.

"First they have to find us. Jayda won't be making the same mistake with her father again. No one knows we're here."

"The place is too easily accessible, though," Oliver remarked. "Someone is bound to remark on your presence eventually."

"And not all of us can hide in plain sight," Adrian

said with a sigh. "Which means Emma might not have a choice."

"Choice about what?"

"Her horn. It is the thing that most stands out. Xiu and my dear Jane can wear glasses or contacts to hide their eyes. The twins can bathe inside. But unless we restrict Emma to her room..." Adrian shrugged.

"You can't make her a prisoner."

"Then the horn must go."

"She says it always grows back."

"Which means she'll require almost daily amputation."

The word made him wince. Funny how when Oliver had first met her, he'd offered to find her a doctor to do just that. Now, telling Emma she had to remove it felt all kinds of wrong.

"Will it hurt her?"

"A bit. But not for long. We've shorn it down before while she was sedated. She wakes with no ill effect. Although I forbade it after the second time it was done. It didn't seem right to keep removing it."

"Then why do it in the first place?"

"Would you believe Aloysius, the man you know as Dr. Cerberus, had this strange notion that it might have healing properties? I told him he'd read too many fairy tales."

"I take it there was nothing magical about it."

Adrian shrugged. "Not that I was ever told, but apparently, Aloysius had more secrets than I realized."

"When are you going to tell Emma it's got to be

cut?" Oliver asked, only to shake his head. "You know what, let me tell her. That is, if it's okay I tell her about Cerberus and stuff."

"Go ahead. Perhaps understanding why we're asking will make it easier for her."

Except, when he went to her room and knocked, there was no answer. Probably already in bed. He went to move away when he heard voices. As he moved in the direction of the pool, the voices grew louder.

"What part of not interested do you not grasp?" he heard Emma say, her exasperation clear.

"Not like you can be choosy. Or are you going to claim you're a lesbian? Is that blind chick more your style?" That was Jacob, being an ass as usual.

"Just because I'm not interested in you doesn't mean I don't like men. I just don't like you."

"You know what, I really don't give a flying fuck. I'm tired of jerking off in the shower," Jacob said crudely.

"Let go of me."

Oliver drew near enough to see Jacob holding Emma by the arm roughly. Yanking on her. Drawing a sharp cry of pain.

It roused the hero in him. "Hey, asshole, you heard the lady. She's not interested."

He drew Jacob's attention and sneer. "Fuck off, meat sack. This doesn't concern you, so walk away."

Except Oliver wasn't about to walk away. "Emma is my concern, and you're hurting her. Let her go."

"Or what? Do you really want to go toe to toe with

me?" Jacob shoved at Emma and sent her stumbling. He strutted up to Oliver, chest puffed out, his eyes glowing a sickly yellow.

"I am not going to let you hurt her." While acutely aware he didn't have a weapon, Oliver didn't back down.

"But I am going to hurt you." Jacob lunged, his fist catching Oliver in the gut, driving the breath out of him.

He managed to suck in a lungful of air and duck the next swing before tossing a jab, the blow blocked by Jacob, who wore a cruel smile.

"I am going to enjoy grinding your face in the dirt and forcing you to listen while I make pony girl scream."

The idea Jacob would hurt Emma adrenalized him. Oliver rushed Jacob, slamming into the other guy, exchanging blows. Problem was, while he felt each and every shot, it didn't look like anything he landed was slowing the other guy down.

On the contrary, the more Oliver hit him, the more energized Jacob became. Bigger, too. The man not only bulked up but his teeth became more pronounced. Oliver sucked in a breath when a rapid swing he couldn't avoid scored a line of fire across his chest. Somehow, Jacob now sported claws that sliced.

"Leave him alone," Emma yelled, running at Jacob, her eyes glowing with a silvery purple hue, kind of like her horn, in the scant starlight outside.

"Don't worry, pony girl. Your turn is next."

"Like fuck," said a new addition to their party. Jett arrived wearing his habitual glower. "You." He jabbed a finger at Jacob. "Get your ass back to your room before I shove your head so far up it you'll see what you ate for lunch last week."

"You can't tell me what to do," Jacob yelled, spittle flying around the guttural words. "I'll fuck you up, too, and then show your wife what a real man feels like—"

Wham. Jett moved so fast even Jacob never saw the fist coming. The asshole hit the ground and tried to roll to his knees to rise. Jett showed no mercy and kicked him. Hard.

Jacob coughed. "Motherfucker. You can't do this. You're not even one of us."

"And yet take a guess who Chimera would keep?" Jett grabbed him by the hair and yanked Jacob to his feet.

"Only because you're fucking the mermaid."

Thump. Jacob's head snapped back as Jett hissed. "Mention my wife again and I'll kill you."

"You can't kill me. Chimera promised me safety."

"I don't care what Adrian promised. I think you're a piece of shit. The world would be a better place without you in it." Jett shoved Jacob from him and watched as he hit the ground hard on his hands and knees. "Get to your fucking room. Now!" he barked.

Jacob shot a belligerent look over his shoulder before scurrying off.

Oliver sighed. "That won't turn out well. You know he's going to retaliate."

"His type always does," Jett remarked with a sneer. "Hopefully we won't have to deal with him much longer. You all right?" Jett asked Emma, not Oliver, the one getting beaten.

"I'm fine. Oliver came to my rescue." She sounded quite bemused by that fact.

"I doubt Jacob will come back, but just in case, I'll walk you to your room," Jett offered.

"No, you have rounds to do. Oliver can escort me." She cast a shy glance at him, and despite his swelling lip, he smiled.

"Whatever. If Jacob bothers you again, let me know. I could use an excuse to beat on his ass." Jett sauntered off, just another shadow in the night, keeping them safe.

Emma stepped close and raised her hand to Oliver's cheek. "I can't believe you came to my rescue."

"I wasn't about to let him hurt you," he hotly declared.

"I can take care of myself."

"You shouldn't have to."

She ducked her head as she whispered, "Thank you."

When she turned from him, rather than let her move away, he captured her hand. "I told Jett I'd walk you to your room."

The feel of her slim fingers laced with his brought a welcome warmth to his chest. "Why were you outside?" he asked when the silence stretched.

"Enjoying the night air. I didn't get out much today."

"Why not?"

"Because I was almost seen by a lost tourist after we chatted this morning. I'm going to have to be more careful about my excursions outdoors."

Since she gave him the opening, he dove in. "You need to cut your horn."

She stiffened, and he almost groaned as he realized he'd blurted it out without giving context. "Don't freak. Because I'm not saying to do it because it's ugly or something. But because you're in danger."

She uttered a dainty snort. "I'm always in danger. Story of my life. Even before the horn, my life sucked."

The quiet despair tugged at him. "I wish things were different for you."

"Wish I didn't have a horn, hunh? Can't say as I blame you."

"What? Wait, that's not what I meant. Listen." He turned her so she faced him, chin tilted, horn held high. "I think you're beautiful. Horn and all."

"Then why tell me I need to cut it?" She couldn't quite stem the hurt in the words.

"Because I want to protect you. But it was a bad idea. I'll find a way to keep you safe. There's got to be something I can do."

She cupped his cheek. "You don't have to be my hero."

"What if I want to be your hero?" And then

because the darkness emboldened him, "What if I want to be more than that?"

"Like what?"

"Your lover."

For a moment, the silence between them stretched, and he wanted to punch himself in the face. She must think him stupid. Or maybe the attraction was one-sided. Or—

Her lips smashed against his and gave him an answer.

CHAPTER FOURTEEN

It was crazy, spontaneous, possibly foolish, and yet the moment Oliver said he wanted to be her lover, she gave up on reining in her heart—and her libido.

Maybe she was making a mistake again. She didn't really care because there was something about this man who'd had the courage to admit he was wrong and change his point of view, who stood up for her when no one else ever did, that made her want any happiness he could give.

This interlude might only last one night or a few days. She wasn't naïve enough to think he'd want to remain with a girl like her forever, but she'd take what she could get.

And enjoy every minute of it.

"We shouldn't be doing this outside," he murmured against her mouth.

He was right. She had a perfectly good bed not far. She dragged him over to her door, keeping their lips locked, afraid he'd change his mind. Yet he stumbled into her room and kicked the door shut, his mouth latched to hers. His breath hot. His hands everywhere.

He wasn't alone in touching.

It had been so long since she'd desired anyone. She'd almost resigned herself to never enjoying intimacy with someone again.

But what she felt with Oliver was more than simple carnal need. He enflamed her. His presence. His kiss. The touch of his fingers as they slid under her shirt.

All of her ached for more, which was why she began tearing at his clothes.

"Let me turn on a light," he said.

The light would bare her to him. She wasn't ready for that. "We don't need light when we can use our touch." She tugged on his shirt, pulling it up and over his chest. A chest she still remembered dripping wet when he'd bathed in the lake.

She kissed his pectorals as he tugged the shirt over his head. Played with the hard nipples, raked her nails down the firm flesh, drawing a groan from him.

She shoved at him. The backs of his knees hit the bed, and he sat down hard. She knelt between his legs, the shadows in the room deep because of the drawn curtains, but she could still see. See his shaft jutting from his groin, eager for her touch.

It required her being careful with the angle of her head. Wouldn't want to gore him by accident. She wrapped her fingers around him and stroked up and down, feeling the hardness of him, the arousal.

"Emma." He murmured her name, and it brought a shiver to her skin. He knew who touched him.

Wanted her to caress him.

She squeezed her hand tight, and a groan escaped him. A peek showed him with his head tilted back. A man enjoying himself.

She dragged a nail over the tip of his cock, a tease that caused him to jerk. A bead of fluid leaked from the tip. She lapped at the drop before swirling her tongue around the thick head. That drew another groan, which, in turn, caused a frisson of pleasure between her legs.

Sitting sideways, she lapped the head of his cock thoroughly before licking her way down to the root of him. She worked her way back up then down again, wetting every inch, making it slippery enough for her hand to easily glide.

His hips twitched and then bucked as she took the tip of his cock into her mouth. She gave him a hard suck, and he inhaled a sharp breath. She worked more of him into her mouth, wondering how much of his big cock she could take.

Not all of it, that was for sure. She needed her hand to cover a good portion of it.

She suctioned his shaft, bobbing her head up and

down while stroking him with her hand. A shudder went through him, and a long, low groan escaped him.

She could have sucked him to completion, but her tingling pussy protested. Standing between his legs, she pulled off her shirt.

He kissed her belly, his own hands working at her pants, pulling them down over her hips, his face in line with that most intimate part of her.

When he'd pulled off her pants, he tugged her close, rubbing his face against her. But it was the hand he slid between her thighs, stroking against her nether lips, that had her gasping and digging her nails into his shoulders to stay upright.

"You are so wet," he murmured, sliding a finger into her. She arched, holding tight to him as he worked that finger in and out.

"I need you." The simple yet urgent truth. She shoved at him until he lay on the bed, and then she straddled him, her heated core hovering atop his straining cock. She lowered herself until he could rub against her.

"Tease," he grumbled, grabbing hold of her hips.

"Is this better?" she asked, pushing herself onto him, loving how he stretched her.

"God, Emma. Oh God." She wasn't even fully seated, and yet he was close to losing control.

The realization almost made her come. She shoved herself fully onto his cock, the pleasure of it making her head tilt back.

For a moment she sat on him, feeling the throbbing of his shaft buried deep. Pleasurable, but she wanted to come.

She began to rock on him, rolling her body atop him, grinding herself hard and pushing him deep. So deep he rubbed against something that made her channel tighten. Her breathing turned ragged. His thumb reached between them and found her clit, rubbed it as she pounded against him.

She cried out his name as she climaxed. She would have fallen on him if he hadn't rolled her so she lay on her back beneath him, their bodies still connected.

He thrust into her, his long strokes drawing out her bliss, stretching her taut again. When he whispered, "Come for me again, Emma. I want to feel you squeezing me tight," she obeyed and came hard.

He came with her, his cock driving deep one last time and pulsing inside her.

A reminder they'd not used protection.

And she didn't care. If he left her pregnant, then at least she'd have someone to love when he left her.

He collapsed by her side but drew her close.

"What are you thinking?" he asked.

"That it's been a while, and if you can handle it, I'd like to do it again."

They did it again more slowly. And once more when they woke in the morning. They would have spent the day in bed, but Oliver claimed they needed food.

But that night, as soon as supper ended, they fled to the privacy of her room, where he made her body sing. Made her believe that maybe, just maybe, they could find a way to make this work.

The sound of cars screaming into the parking lot shattered that dream.

CHAPTER FIFTEEN

Screaming tires and slamming doors never boded well in any circumstance. Having been in a few war zones, Oliver reacted quickly, rolling out of bed, dragging Emma with him.

"Stay down," he advised as he snared his pants and yanked them on.

"What's happening?" she asked.

"I don't know. Let me go find out."

He stepped outside barefoot, his shirt untucked, still smelling of sex. But there was no time for a shower. There might not even be time for goodbyes, given the guns trained on him the moment he popped out of the door of the motel.

So many guns.

"On your knees!" shouted a guy, his face hidden behind a black mask. All of them hid their features and wore the gear of an attack force.

Lacing his hands behind his head, Oliver obeyed,

hitting the ground on his knees, hoping Emma remained inside.

"Who are you?" he asked. Obviously, a group who'd planned well seeing as how the most capable fighters weren't around. Jayda and Marcus had left because of a tip. While Adrian, Jane, and Jett popped off overnight to deal with some other business. How convenient.

"We'll be asking the questions. Where are the women and children?"

The demand made his blood run cold. "I don't know what you're talking about. Just me staying here. Thinking of turning this place into a nudist resort."

The guy shouting the orders drew near, the barrel of his weapon even with Oliver's face. "Think you're funny?"

"Not really. But I've been called bluntly poetic in a review. Name is Oliver Marshall," he announced. "You might have heard of me. Famous author. Someone who will be missed if you kill me or try and stuff me in some hidden installation."

"I don't give a fuck who you are. We didn't come for you. Where are the others?"

"I told you—"

The shriek of an angry child pierced the air. More than likely Margaret trying to keep Lorcan quiet, not something that busy boy would like.

The man in front of him probably smirked under his mask. "Search the rooms. Find those children. Take anybody you find."

"No." The exclamation came from Emma, which meant—

"Holy shit. That woman has a horn!"

"That woman is my girlfriend," Oliver muttered, diving at the distracted leader. He hit him in the midsection and managed to put him off balance, but his real objective was getting his hands on the gun.

Which turned out to be full of tranquilizers he realized the moment he fired the first shot. Bullet or not, it did the trick, taking the guy down before he could retaliate. However, there were so many more bad guys to go.

And none of them were intent on him.

Emma came prancing out of the motel room, which sounded odd, but there was something quite wild and beautiful in the way she galloped at the soldiers sent to take them in.

Her hair flowed behind her, and she ducked her head, horn leading the way. Surely she—

He gulped as she speared a man only moments after he fired on her.

The fellow slid off her horn as she pulled back, the length of it glistening with blood. She rubbed her foot on the ground, her eyes a maelstrom of silver and purple rage.

"Emma?"

She didn't even look at him as she charged the next victim. His attention was distracted by the crashing of glass as a little hellion came soaring through. Followed a moment later by his father.

No more did Luke just look like a rugged, unkempt kind of guy. He'd gone feral, his body big and his teeth huge. He grabbed his son and tucked him under an arm before tearing into a soldier.

Lorcan didn't cooperate. He wiggled free and hit the ground, helping his dad by latching onto an attacker's ankle.

Margaret chose that moment to emerge, screaming for her baby. "Get back here, Lorcan. Let daddy handle it."

She should have stayed inside. Her humanity was no match for the dart that hit her and put her instantly to sleep. *It's a wonder I'm still standing*, Oliver thought as he stared down at the tuft sticking out of his arm.

He yanked it free. Must have been a dud.

Emma still chased after the attackers, sporting more than a few darts. Adrenaline kept her going, but she wouldn't be able to prevail against the numbers. He tried to help, shooting at the soldiers, cursing when his darts hit their heavy vests and didn't penetrate farther.

It was kind of insulting how they ignored his efforts.

Things looked dire, and then Becky stepped out of her room. She looked ethereal in that moment, her hair flowing down over shoulders, her arms spread wide as she broke into song.

A song that stopped the fighting.

Everyone swayed where they stood, even Luke.

So beautiful. Pure. They didn't want to fight.

Weapons fell to the ground in a clatter. People followed next, kneeling before the siren and her song.

Only one thing marred the music, the discordant clack of heels, the muttered, "Must I do everything myself?" The *pft* sound as a dart was fired and fired again. And again.

He gaped, eyes wide in disbelief.

Becky stared down at her chest then let out a strident cry that burst more than a few ears before crumpling.

Head ducked, he clutched his ears as they pulsed with pain.

The pointed toes of the shoes appeared before he heard anything through the ringing in his head. He stared at them and thought, *No, it can't be.*

Yet the sinking sensation in his belly didn't lie. He looked up and saw her. The bane of his existence wearing earphones to muffle noise—and song.

"You just couldn't leave it alone, could you?" The words were said with disdain.

Oliver sighed. "Hello, Mother."

"Mother?" Emma slurred the word and blinked a few times, trying to hold her head high.

"I'm sorry," he apologized as Emma turned to him, betrayal in her gaze. She passed out before he could say, "I had nothing to do with it."

"Of course, you didn't. God forbid you do something useful for once in your life." His mother scowled at him.

"Why are you here?"

"Isn't it obvious?"

His mother, who removed the protection over her ears, smiled as she turned and faced Luke, who was rising despite the obvious lethargy in his body.

She fired her gun. More darts. Obviously stronger ones than those her men bore.

Luke hit the ground, mumbling, "Bitch."

He didn't know the half of it. Oliver wasn't surprised at all when she turned to him and took aim.

"I'll see you back at the house, where you belong."

Pft.

CHAPTER SIXTEEN

OLIVER WOKE FASTER THAN HE WOULD HAVE expected given he was darted. As promised, he was home again, a prisoner who could only pace his bedroom—his childhood bedroom. Not that it was ever a child-friendly place. The walls were covered in patterned navy blue paper, trimmed at the floor and around the windows and doors with mahogany-varnished wood. A room more suitable for an adult or a temporary guest. Which Oliver technically was.

Most of his childhood was spent at boarding schools. He only came home for summer break and Christmas holiday. Mother believed children should be rarely seen, never heard, and didn't have much use for him until he'd graduated from college.

Only by then, he had no interest in her or the family business. If only she'd lose all interest in him.

Was he the reason she'd attacked that motel? Had

she finally located her missing maternal instinct and gone looking for her son?

Doubtful.

He rolled out of bed as he replayed that awful scene in the motel parking lot. She'd sent her mercenaries ahead, armed with weak tranquilizers. Why?

For a moment he saw Lorcan's drooling grin.

Because of the children. She'd come prepared to knock them out, too. The cold calculation of it had him pacing, twenty strides, pivot. Twenty strides, pivot. His room loomed larger than his first apartment. But he'd have taken that shithole he paid for working two jobs any day over this cold mausoleum of a house.

When he'd left, he'd sworn to never return. And she'd practically shouted good riddance.

But then his older brother died, which left only Oliver as heir to her empire. They were both disappointed.

He cared less about failing to live up to his mother's expectations than the fact Emma thought he was responsible for the attack. He'd seen the expression on her face. The betrayal in her eyes before the drugs took effect.

Emma, the woman he'd made love to, who rescued spiders from indoors and relocated them outside. Who wouldn't eat meat.

Gored that man with her horn...

But could he really condemn her for protecting herself? If he'd had a real gun, he would have used it.

As it was, he'd only had his fists and the tranquilizer pistol he stole. And they weren't enough.

Mother had come prepared, which made him wonder how long she'd planned this. She'd timed her attack well. With Jayda and Marcus off saving a patient, and Chimera doing something with Jane and Jett, they were at their weakest. Either someone was watching their every move or their hidden group had a Judas.

Problem was they probably assumed that traitor was Oliver. He couldn't exactly blame them for the erroneous assumption given his attitude with them initially stunk and he wasn't in a cage, though he'd wager they were. Probably in the same facility where he'd conducted his interviews with the other patients and Cerberus himself.

"Damn you, Mother," he muttered as he stomped back and forth. A prisoner until she chose to set him free. He'd already tried the door—locked. The windows didn't need bars, given the third-floor setting made it impossible to jump and the smooth exterior wall made It impossible to descend, unless he jumped.

How ironic and frustrating that he'd ended up in the clutches of the person he was trying to destroy. His mother, probably the biggest monster of all. More so because she was completely human. She had no excuse for the things she did.

The sons she neglected.

The drugs she overcharged for.

The people she kept prisoner in the hopes of using them to make even more money.

It was only by accident Oliver discovered his mother had gotten her hands on Cerberus and other Chimera patients. She'd tried to keep them hidden from him and almost succeeded until the anonymous tip. It was at that point Oliver made a convincing argument about letting him interview Cerberus and the others as research for his book. Her vanity let her believe him when he lied and claimed the narrative he planned to pen would mark the triumph of her company when it became the number one pharmaceutical company in the world.

She thought he'd finally come around to her way of thinking. Little did she know his plan was to take the company down. And her with it.

There was no love between him and his mother. She often referred to him as "the mistake." For years she'd ignored the existence of her youngest son, until his older brother died in an accident, making Oliver the only heir. She dragged him back practically kicking and screaming after first getting him fired from the network that engaged him to write a documentary on the drug problem in America. She got all his credit cards cancelled, kicked out of his apartment, and car repossessed.

Oliver was practically starving when he finally gave in and came home. But only because he was determined to break free.

Some might think him callous for the way he hated his mother. They'd obviously never met her.

He whirled at the sound of a key in the lock. His mother entered, looking as composed as ever in a pantsuit made of black linen, the blouse a crimson splash of color. Her hair had gone from the light blonde of his youth to a silver bob that framed her angular face. A pretty woman if you ignored the cold calculation in her eyes and the ever-present disdain on her lips.

"Let me out of this room," was the first thing he said.

"Is that any way to greet your mother?" she asked.

"You had me darted and carted off like livestock." Oliver clenched his hands by his side, seething with rage.

"What did you expect? Really, Oliver, when you went off on that expedition of yours, I expected you to infiltrate their operation, not become one of them."

The statement and its meaning sank in slowly. "You knew I wasn't on vacation."

"Did you really think otherwise?" The curl of her lip told him he'd been an idiot. "I knew from the start when you asked to write that book that you were planning a coup against me."

"So why didn't you stop me?"

She arched a perfectly coiffed brow. "Stop one of the greatest investigative journalists of his time? Who better to ferret out any remaining Chimera projects than my own son?"

"You used me." Used him to get at Emma and the others.

"About time you were useful."

"What have you done with Emma?"

"I assume you mean the girl with the horn. Interesting creature that one. But not the one I'd hoped to nab. Unfortunately, my true objective skipped out before my men arrived."

"Let me guess, you wanted Dr. Chimera."

"Him and his companion, Jane. A woman who can not only walk through fire but call it and use it. Do you have any idea how many governments would pay to have soldiers with that ability? And even better, given how besotted Chimera is with her, he would have fallen into our grasp as well. But it wasn't a complete loss. We might not have gotten all of them, but we managed to capture the mermaid and her spawn, the unicorn, and the wolfman."

"How did you know where to find us?"

"A rat within your midst." His mother smirked. "It only takes one."

"Who?" Who betrayed them?

At first, he thought his mother wouldn't answer, but she smirked. "They think you did. After all, why else would the son and heir of Leyghas Labs have come looking for the Chimaeram Clinic in the first place?"

"You told them who I was." He'd expected it and yet deflated at the claim.

"I had to, seeing as how you neglected to inform them. Really, Oliver, have some pride in your family."

"I hate my family." It was why he'd kept his father's surname rather than take his mother's when she had hers legally changed.

"What did I do to get stuck with you?" The shake of her head spoke of her disappointment. "It should have been you that died in that car crash and not Xavier." The favored elder son whose car went off a cliff and was never found.

"Your love warms the heart, Mother." He'd long ago given up expecting anything from her. "Where have you taken Emma and the others?"

"The same place as we're keeping Cerberus. Think Chimera will take the bait and attempt a rescue?"

Probably, because no way would Jett allow the kidnapping of his wife and daughters to pass. "You shouldn't have taken them." Oliver shook his head and began pacing again. "Chimera will come. And he won't be alone. You have to evacuate the lab."

"Why would I do that?" She smirked.

"Because people will die."

"Such pessimism. I'm ready for whatever they might bring. Looking forward to it actually. Let them show the watching cameras what they're capable of. Then we'll know what aspects we want to harness and sell."

"I'm going to stop you."

"No, you won't." His mother shook her head. "You are about to become the son I need."

"Never."

"Did you know," she said, as if he'd never spoken, "that we've already begun trials on the new serum?"

"What?"

"Discreetly of course. Some bums we gathered from the streets that no one will miss. A good thing since they've failed so far." She scowled, more disturbed by the serum not working than the fact she'd killed people.

"You need to stop."

"Why would we stop? We are on the cusp of the biggest discovery in the world. We will stop all the pain and suffering."

"And rake in billions with no care to the consequences or side effects." Oliver shook his head. "The Chimera treatment isn't ready. It may never be ready."

"You better hope that's not the case, or I won't have any use for your friends."

As she moved to leave, he blurted out, "What are you going to do with me?"

"That depends on you. Either you're with me or—"

He lunged at her. With his size, it should have been easy to knock her down and escape his room.

But mother always was one step ahead.

The Taser she hit him with sent him to the floor jiggling, but he still heard her say, "Take him to the lab. I hear they've just mixed up a new batch for us to try."

CHAPTER SEVENTEEN

EMMA WASN'T TOO SURPRISED TO WAKE IN A CAGE. Once again, she'd put her faith in someone and they'd screwed her over. Thing was this time really hurt.

She'd trusted Oliver. Believed him when he claimed he'd changed his mind about her. She'd shared not only her body with him but her fragile heart.

And he'd stomped all over it.

He'd played her all along. Played them all. Now they paid the price.

Rising from her cot, she took stock of her location. The word bleak came to mind, but it was clean. Everything appeared shiny and new, from the freshly painted concrete wall at the back of her cell to the soldered metal bars that were sunk into the concrete floor and ceiling. The drain in the middle of her floor had a shiny cap and wasn't large enough to squeeze through. Hers wasn't the only cage. A line of them spanned the room, two rows facing each other with each cell possessing a gap between them wide enough that she'd wager if she stretched out her hand, she wouldn't even be able to touch the fingertips of the person in the cell next to hers.

"Luke?" She noticed him in the cage beside hers, sitting lotus style on the floor, glaring across and to his left at his wife, who lay prone on a cot. Without her son.

"Oh shit," she muttered. She didn't dare ask aloud if Margaret was dead. Luke surely wouldn't be so calm if that were the case. As she watched, Margaret's chest rose and fell. She lived.

"Don't touch the bars," he advised.

She almost asked why, and then she heard it, that steady humming buzz that indicated current. Whoever took them prisoner didn't want them escaping.

What do you mean whoever? Ollie and his mom conspired against us.

Straight across from Luke was another cage, big enough to hold a clear vat filled with liquid. She could see Becky floating in it. Her baby daughters huddled close.

On Emma's other side there was Jacob, who paced and mumbled, "Fucking lied to me."

She could understand his anger. Oliver had lied to them all.

"Fucking bitch. She promised me a fresh start. Not a fucking cage."

Jacob's words caught her attention. "What did you say?"

His sulking gaze turned her way. "I said I'm not supposed to be in here. She said if I turned you in, I could go free."

Luke sprang to his feet and approached the bars but didn't grip them. "You're the one that fucked us over and gave them our location?"

"I didn't have a choice. It was the only way they'd let me go."

"Who? Who captured you?" Emma asked.

"The bitch running Leyghas Labs. Maudette Leyghas. She had her lawyers spring me from the police station after they arrested me for stealing food but only so she could imprison me and use me as a guinea pig."

"You told them all about us," said Luke with a sneer.

"Not me. They already knew everything. Even knew who else crashed on the helicopter with me. When I told them Emma was alive..." He shrugged. "They made me a deal. Said I could go free if I helped them find Emma or any of the other mutants."

"We're not mutants."

Jacob sneered. "Yeah, we are. Especially you." Said pointedly at Emma. "For some reason they were real interested in you. They dangled me as bait, hoping someone from the clinic would come after me."

"And we went for it," Luke growled, disgusted by the trap.

Emma frowned. "But nothing happened for a week. Why did they wait so long?"

"Because there were more of you than expected. So they waited until the scariest and most dangerous of the group were gone. Only then did they swoop in."

"I was still around," growled Luke listening in.

"But the others weren't and that provided an opening."

"You let them know when we were at our weakest," Emma stated.

"I had to. I made a deal."

"Fucking moron. Did you seriously believe they'd keep their word?" Luke snorted.

Emma could understand the disdain. "Was Oliver part of it?"

That brought a shrug from Jacob. "Probably. I mean he is her son."

Not exactly an answer. Was it possible he had nothing to do with it? She squashed that hope before it could fully bloom.

"What do they want with us?" she asked instead.

"What everyone wants. To know the secrets to our greatness." The deep voice had them turning and noticing a cage at the far end of the room. A larger cell than theirs with many creature comforts to keep the devil within happy.

"Dr. Cerberus?" There was a lilt in Emma's query, mostly because she barely recognized the man. Horns jutted from his forehead, and while his skin remained dark, it had a texture to it, kind of scaly. He was also much larger. Bulkier. Taller, too, given, when he stood, his head practically brushed the top of his cage. And were those wings at his back?

"Ah, if it isn't our lucky little unicorn. I was delighted to hear they'd found you. You and all our other successes. Especially the babies." The grin on his face had too many teeth and a subtle undercurrent of malice.

Luke snapped. "Motherfucker, I'm going to kill you."

"Is that any way to greet the doctor who helped save you?" Cerberus chided.

"Luke, what's happening?" Margaret chose that moment to rouse, and Luke hurried to speak to her, but Emma was more interested in Cerberus.

"How long have you been a prisoner?" Emma asked.

"Prisoner? I came here of my own free will," Cerberus boasted.

"Says the demon in the locked cell," Luke muttered.

"A minor misunderstanding. I've allowed it for the moment, because they are giving me what I want."

"What do you want?" Emma asked.

"World domination." He said it so seriously she almost believed him, but then Cerberus laughed. "The expression on your face is quite priceless."

"Any idea what they are going to do to us?" she asked.

"I imagine Luke with his fighting skills will be

copied for the military. Becky and her daughters shall help spawn a new species that will live in the oceans, easing the burden of life on Earth."

"What of me?" Jacob blurted. "They promised me freedom."

Cerberus turned a yellow-slitted gaze his way. "You? You already served your purpose bringing those with true worth to us. I imagine there is a dissection in your future."

"What?" Jacob hollered before making the mistake of grabbing the electrified bars. He hit the floor twitching. It made her wonder if part of his hybrid mix included a worm.

Emma was almost afraid to find out what they had in store for her. It worried her so much that her horn—longer than it ever had been—began to ache.

As if he read her mind, Dr. Cerberus—who truly looked like the devil when he turned his freaky gaze in her direction—said, "They'll try and make more of you, my lucky little unicorn. They will try and fail. Funny thing about some of our more mythical recreations. It's not just genetics that decide the final shape. There is something in the aura. Something that is a part of you that can't be replicated. A shame given the special properties of your horn."

"What about my horn?" she asked as it ached even more fiercely.

It wasn't Cerberus who answered. A door slid open and drew attention as a woman, dressed in a slim black pencil skirt and dark jacket, entered. Her hair was a strict silver bob that went well with the flat expression in her eyes while her blouse matched the blood-red lipstick. "Your horn is about to make my company billions."

"I don't understand." Emma couldn't help but recognize the woman, the same one Oliver called mother. The person who'd put them all in cages.

"Of course you don't understand, because the lovely doctors at the clinic never told you." The woman strutted toward her, the clack of her heels drawing a low, rumbling growl from Luke.

He looked quite feral as he glared through the bars. "What have you done with my son?"

"He's currently running tests. Literally. Endurance. Agility. Although, it took us a bit of convincing before he obeyed. Savage little beast."

"He's a baby!" Margaret exclaimed.

"Hardly a baby. Despite his linear age, physically he's more of a toddler and definitely in the terrible stage. We'll have to ensure those who train him use a firm hand to keep him in line."

Luke slammed into the bars and, despite the sizzle, managed to snarl. "You bitch! Give me back my son."

"I don't think so. Your boy is about to become our poster child for the future. With his projected rate of growth, he'll reach adulthood in less than half the time of an unmodified person. Think of it. Only a decade to build an army of super soldiers. Less time if we treat full-grown adults. Although we'll have to find a way to make you more malleable." The woman sneered in Luke's direction. "I hear shock collars are effective in controlling a dog's bark."

He grabbed the bars, ignoring the current running through them, his hair standing on end, his body vibrating with the electricity "You'll pay for this."

"No, she will if you don't behave." The woman pointed to Margaret, and Luke's face turned ashen as he stepped back from the bars. A wolfman brought to heel by his love for his wife.

"Why are you doing this?" Emma asked.

"Didn't Oliver spill the beans? I thought for sure that poor excuse for a son would have whined about my plan." The red lips curled. "You know, if it weren't for the DNA test proving he was mine, I'd wonder if he got switched at birth. Such a disappointment he turned out to be."

"If he's so disappointing, then why did you use him to capture us?" Jacob took credit, but to dispel any remaining doubt, Emma needed to know once and for all if Oliver was involved.

"You think Oliver helped? I wish he had the balls." Maudette Leyghas laughed. "Oliver tried to talk me out of my plans. He thought I didn't know he was sneaking around, gathering company secrets, intent on revealing them to the world. As if I would allow him to do that. My company is on the cusp of making billions, maybe even trillions, of dollars."

"What you're doing is illegal."

"Only if someone finds out." The top lip pulled back in a sneer. "And I've made sure that won't happen."

"Are you the one responsible for the attacks on us?" Luke asked.

"You mean the raid on the clinic and then Chimera's house? Piss-poor operations." She shook her head. "Not me, but we were watching and we learned from Romanov's mistakes. His problem was he went in like a bull in a china shop, thinking he could just smash and take. We observed. Gathered intel. Retrieved the projects that surfaced. Imagine our delight when we found out the world's only unicorn survived. Because of you, I'll become the most powerful woman in the world."

"You're evil," Emma stated.

"How funny. That's exactly what Oliver said before I had him strapped to a table."

Her blood ran cold. "What did you do to him?"

"Me?" An exaggerated innocence that turned into a sneer. "Nothing. Yet. But it won't be long. I'd already started a mild course of treatments before he took off on his ill-advised expedition. And now that he's returned, it's time to finish them."

"You're experimenting on your son?" Emma couldn't help but be appalled.

"A mother must do what she has to in order to gain the son she needs. And don't act so shocked. After all, you're the reason why it's even possible. You and that lovely horn of yours." Maudette snapped her fingers, and some of the guards who'd stood silent at her back moved forward. "Part of the problem with the Chimera treatments was the length of time needed to implement them. Not to mention the pain. Hard to sell a cure that hurts more than the disease or impairment or that requires placing subjects in extended comas. But it turns out the legends are true. A unicorn horn does have power. A secret even Chimera never knew. But Cerberus did. Becky was his first real success."

"What are you talking about?" Luke appeared puzzled. "I thought she stole some of Chimera's cure and took it."

"She did, and would have died with that alone. The human body wasn't supposed to be able to adapt that quickly."

Cerberus interceded, rumbling, "Which is why Becky also got more than few thermoses of broth, thickened with the fine ground powder of a horn."

Emma's touched her horn, shaking as realization hit. "They cut it on purpose."

"Don't whine," Maudette snapped. "It grew back. And it better keep growing back because we're going to need lots of it. Starting now. Bring her to the operation room."

"What? No." Emma backed up in her cage and hit the wall because there was nowhere to go. Nowhere to run and hide.

The black spots danced. Her breathing huffed hotly through her nose, and a foot rubbed on the floor.

"She's gonna charge."

"Tranq her!" someone yelled.

They must have drugged her good, because despite rushing toward the bars, she didn't recall hitting them. And when she woke, her horn was gone.

CHAPTER EIGHTEEN

Oliver woke strapped to a bed, which wasn't exactly his idea of a good time. Especially since he could see the light overhead, the big kind used in operating rooms.

It especially boded ill, given his last recollection involved his mother saying something to the effect of, "Since you love the monsters so much, you'll be glad to know you're already becoming one."

What the hell was that supposed to mean? Except he had a funny feeling he knew. The flu shot the company made him get. The nights he slept deeper and longer than usual, waking in the afternoon rather than the ass crack of dawn.

How long had his mother been screwing with him? Experimenting on her own son?

The realization made his blood run cold and, at the same time, ignited a heated panic. He struggled against the restraints, only to quickly realize he wasn't going anywhere. Was this how Emma and the others felt when they were being treated? Helpless. Terrified.

Excited.

What?

It surprised him to find a kernel of anticipation within. A part of him wondered what kind of super power he'd get. Strength or speed? Would he appear rugged and human like Marcus and Luke, or would his genes succumb to the beast and he'd be forever damned to live in shadows?

What if he didn't want to be a monster?

Although, if he did become one, it would make convincing Emma he'd not betrayed her much easier. How could she ever forgive him? His own mother conspired against her. Captured her. Even now, probably hurt her.

Thinking of the devil conjured his mother. He heard her heels and smelled her perfume before she neared enough for him to perceive her.

"Bitch," he hissed.

Mother didn't actually look at him but rather at the doctor with his abnormally large syringe, the liquid within glinting with a silvery sheen. Sparkly almost like Emma's horn.

A pit formed in his stomach the longer he stared. Surely not...

"He's awake already," his mother stated.

"That last dose we gave him before he set off on his trip must have amped up his changes. I'll make a notation in his chart to increase the dosage in the sedative we give him."

"You might want to triple whatever you're planning since the serum we're giving him today promises to be extra potent. We finally got our hands on more of that secret ingredient."

"Let me go," Oliver snapped, straining once more. "I never gave permission for you to do this to me."

Finally, she turned her flat gaze his way. "I'm your mother. That's all the permission I need."

"What have you done to me?"

"I told you. I'm finally making you into a son I can be proud of."

"By turning me into a monster?" His lips stretched into a smile. "Aren't you worried I'll come back to bite you?"

"That wouldn't be a smart move on your part. If you're lucky, my good genes will prevail and you'll be a success story."

"Then I guess I'm fucked since you're a monster already," he snapped.

"Such ingratitude," she said with a fake sniff. "And after all I've done for you."

"You're a hateful, cold-hearted bitch. I would have been better off orphaned than raised by the likes of you."

His mother's face pinched. "Watch your mouth, Oliver. You seem to forget who is in charge."

"How could I when you're constantly reminding me? But here's the thing. I don't care. At one point you'll have to release me, and when you do, I'm coming for you. I will destroy you, and this company."

"If I ever release you," she said with a smirk. She turned to the doctor. "Hurry up and inject him. Let's see if the freshness of Cerberus's special ingredient does make a difference."

"Yes, ma'am." The doctor, a non-descript idiot who never learned to say no, scurried forward with his big needle.

"Don't," Oliver begged, hating the word even as it slipped off his tongue. "Don't do this."

The doctor ignored him, and Oliver felt the pinch of the needle as it slid into the meaty part of his shoulder. A moment later it was done. At first, he felt nothing.

Perhaps his mother had been bullshitting and had him injected with a placebo to scare him.

"I don't think it worked," he taunted.

His mother frowned. "It should. After all, we showed great success with the old horn we ground up. Which I'll add wasn't easy to find. Most of the leads we followed were fakes."

"What horn?"

She ignored him. "Give him another shot."

"But, ma'am—"

"I said—You know what? Never mind. I'll do it myself." She grabbed another syringe out of a fridge and jabbed him with it. The same arm.

"You can't do this. Chimera already said Cerberus was in the dark about the whole treatment process."

"He was, but I figured it out." His mother grinned. "Although, I will admit, the first few subjects we injected didn't fare too well. But then we finally got our hands on some authentic unicorn horn. Old stuff. Brittle and weak. We had our first success."

"Who?"

"No one you need to worry about. He gave his body to science."

He gaped.

"You, on the other hand, are living proof it works."

"Does it?" he taunted. "Because I feel nothing." As if to mock him, a tingling began. It started in his arm, the one he'd gotten the shot in, and ran down to his fingers. With each breath he took, every pump of his heart, the blood carrying the serum travelled through his body until every inch of him vibrated. He began to tremble visibly.

"It's working. How do you feel?" His mother leaned over him, the avarice in her eyes rousing something inside him. Hatred, which he expected, but also a hunger.

"I could use a snack," he grumbled, his voice deeper. He flexed his fingers and made a fist, noticing they felt thicker. The bands around his chest and wrists and ankles, tighter. As if he'd swollen.

Or gotten bigger.

"Look at him. He's changing already," his mother crowed, pleasure in her tone. "This is absolutely wonderful. We need to test it on some more of our subjects."

"We have only enough to do maybe two more."

"Two?" she exclaimed.

"As per your wishes, we kept part of the horn sample for the diagnostic team."

His mother frowned. "How long before the girl grows back that horn long enough to be cut again?"

"What did you say?" Oliver heard his mother's words despite the ringing in his ears.

A familiar smirk hovered over him. "You can thank your girlfriend for the serum already working in your body. Seems a little unicorn horn goes a long way toward making the body accept the treatment. No more need for year-long comas to combat the pain. No more taking it slow. All we need is a chunk of horn mixed in to make everything work better."

"You cut Emma's horn?" he asked quietly.

"Cut it down to the skin. And as soon as it grows back, we'll do it again and again." The big smile held no hint of remorse.

"You cut her horn." Stated this time.

"She didn't take it too well when she woke up," his mother mocked.

Meanwhile, his rage grew, and the bands on his body tightened. "Where is Emma?"

"Not far. You'll see her soon enough when we put you in a cage alongside her. Maybe if you're a good son, I'll allow conjugal visits. Maybe you'll manage to actually do something useful for once and make a child."

"What is wrong with you?" Oliver shouted, trying to lunge, his body held bound.

"I am fulfilling my destiny," his mother spat. "Your father lacked the balls to be great. Didn't have what it took to truly embrace power. And if you don't learn, then once you give me a grandchild, I'll get rid of you like I got rid of him."

"Bitch!" He strained, hard enough that something creaked.

"Um, ma'am. We might want to vacate the room." The doctor looked nervous.

"How about you sedate him instead? Do I have to tell you how to do your job?" she huffed. "Once he's asleep, put him in a cage, the one across from his girlfriend. I'll return tomorrow to check on him."

His mother left, her heels clacking. His rage didn't leave with her. It simmered inside. Whispered to him.

Escape. Save Emma. Save the world.

But how? He pushed again at the restraints. They held, and he could do nothing as the doctor injected him.

Sleep.

He heard the word in his head and wanted to snarl like fuck was he going to close his eyes and...

Hold on a second. Sleep sounded like a good idea. Oliver's lashes fluttered, and his body relaxed. His breathing evened out.

The doctor uttered a sigh of relief. "We better move him now. I don't know how long the drugs will last."

Not long at all sucker.

The bed he lay on jolted into motion as it moved,

and he lay there, quiet as could be, fighting the urge to peek. Not yet.

Time it right.

He'd get only one chance.

There was beeping as a code was entered, the click and clang and whoosh of air as a pressurized door opened.

Then he was assailed with scents and noise...

"Shit, what did you guys do to Ollie?" From Luke.

"Fuck me, that crazy bitch experimented on her own son." Said in a whisper by Jacob.

"I told her the key was in the freshness of the horn." Bloody Cerberus, who'd started this mess with his mother.

But he heard nothing from Emma.

There was the sound of a motor and metal parts moving as they unlocked a cage and the door slid open. Then a bump as they rolled his bed in. Only then did they undo the restraints. He waited until they were done with the second ankle before he moved.

Oliver rolled off the table and threw himself at the first guard, slamming him into the bars, fisting the fabric of his shirt. The guard didn't sizzle indicating the electricity was shut off, and even better the cell door remained open.

He slammed his fist in the man's face and felt a satisfying crunch. He pulled back for another wallop when Luke yelled, "Duck!"

Without hesitation, Oliver dropped to his haunches just in time to see the dart hit the guard, who slumped to the ground. Rather than wait for the guard to correct his aim, Oliver moved, diving for the ankles and taking down the next guard, hearing the panicked third yelling, "Breach. We have a breach. Seal cage seven."

That might have worked better if the guard Oliver was pummeling wasn't lying partially on the track, which meant the sliding door slammed against his head.

The man screamed as the pressure built, and Oliver knew he only had a second. He wedged his body in the gap, his bulk getting stuck. The door kept pushing, and he couldn't seem to budge. The third guard, his eyes wide with fright, aimed a gun at him.

"Becky, now!" Luke shouted.

Oliver found his attention diverted by the sound of falling water, and he turned his head to look. There was a large tank in a massive cage just one cell over from his. Becky and the twins sloshed water over the sides of their tub, spilling it on the floor until it seeped under the bars and pooled under the feet of the guard who fired.

The dart hit Oliver, and he hissed. Not in pain, but because he knew his adrenaline would only work for so long to keep the drugs at bay.

The water stopped sloshing, and Becky bobbed to the surface, a baby in each arm. However, the mother of mermaids had no voice. The gag in her mouth kept her silent.

But nothing was stopping Luke from shouting, "Spit, baby girls. See if you can hit your Uncle Luke."

He might have wondered why, except the moment those little girls squirted a stream of water, ducking and grabbing more in their mouths, that liquid hit Luke's bars with a sizzle and steam. But not all of it evaporated.

As Oliver grunted and shoved at the door still trying to close, and the guard attempted to reload his tranquilizer gun, the girls spat again and connected the puddle on the floor to the electrified bars across from it.

The guard wore boots and didn't fry unfortunately. However, the jolt in the current caused something to pop and blow. The steady hum disappeared.

Luke grinned and grabbed his bars. "Hey, Ollie, wanna wager who gets to him first?"

"The meat sack is mine," Oliver said in a guttural tone he didn't recognize.

"Oliver?" A trembling voice spoke his name. "What happened to you?" Only Emma had the power to draw his attention.

He glanced over and saw Emma rising to her feet, looking wan and fragile. Her hair was a tangled mess around her shoulders, her expression pale, her forehead bloody.

And hornless.

With a roar, Oliver gave a mighty shove and popped free of the door wedging him, stepping on the head of the now quiet guard. Stomping toward the other one that held up his gun in a trembling hand, readying to fire.

"I'll shoot!" said the fellow, stepping back.

Luke grabbed hold and wrenched his head.

Crack.

There was no getting back up from that injury.

A siren blared. There was clanging as doors sealed shut. Sealing them in this section. The vents hissed, and Oliver wanted to scream in frustration.

Luke was the one to talk him down. "Don't worry about the gas. Get me out and I can help."

"How?" he asked, looking at the closed cage door.

"Must I do everything?" Cerberus said in a put-upon tone of voice.

He glanced down the aisle to see Cerberus rise from his seat and put down his book. He could only gape as the demon-man grabbed the bars and pulled at them. Bent them as if they were malleable putty and stepped through.

"Dude, me next!" Luke demanded.

"Didn't you call me a godless devil?" Cerberus asked as the first hints of the gas tickled their noses.

"Water under the bridge, ol' pal." Luke grinned, and Oliver thought for sure the man was done for.

But Cerberus gave him an even more awful smile. "Can't punish a man for speaking the truth."

The devil bent the bars, and Luke stepped out and ran to Margaret's cage. She was pressed against the back wall, her shirt over her mouth and nose. Good plan.

Oliver turned to Emma, only to see her sitting on the floor. He grabbed the bars. "Emma, are you okay? Speak to me."

"Look, Ollie, I'm not a monster anymore." She touched the bloody spot.

"You never were," Oliver exclaimed. "We have to get out of here."

"Why bother?" She shrugged. "They'll just capture me again. I'm the only unicorn in the world, apparently, and they need my horn. They'll never leave me alone."

"Don't you dare give up now," he yelled, slamming his first against the metal. The huge lungful of air meant he breathed in the gas and coughed. His knees weakened, but he held on to the bars.

"I wish we could have had longer," she murmured.

"We can if you get off your ass and come with me." He put his hand through the bars, and she stared at it for a moment.

"You want me?"

"More than anything in this world," he said, his gaze losing focus, his knees weakening. He clung to the bars but still slid down.

"Oh, Ollie." She crept over to him and placed her hand over his.

"Make me puke. Am I the only one who is too smart to succumb to love?" Cerberus grumbled, reaching them and wrenching the bars apart.

He kept on moving past them, headed for the sealed door.

Only Luke and the others were at the opposite end.

"Freedom is this way," Cerberus noted.

"My son is in there." Luke pointed.

In the end, Cerberus wrenched open both doors. He even freed Jacob the traitor. At Luke's urging, Becky, now free to sing, fled with her daughters and Margaret through the door Cerberus claimed led to freedom. But Oliver stuck with Luke, as did Emma.

Someone had to save baby Lorcan.

They had to pass through two labs and a corridor before they found where the baby boy was being held.

Literally.

Luke kicked in the door and roared at the sight of his son tied to a bed.

"Da. Da. Da," Lorcan exclaimed, his voice high and chirping as he strained at the straps holding him down.

"I got you, buddy." Luke made quick work of the restraints and tucked the child against his chest, hugging him, relief warring with rage on his face. "Let's go."

Leave? It was probably best if Luke did, and Emma, too. As for Oliver? "I can't. Not yet. I have something I need to do. Take Emma with you."

Luke gave him a grim nod.

"Wait. Ollie, why aren't you coming?" She glanced back at him as Luke grabbed her by the arm and pulled.

"Go with Luke. I need to have a chat with my

mother." A final one. And he knew just where to find her.

The top-most office belonged to the head of the company. When Oliver stepped through the door, which he demolished with a fire axe he acquired in the hall, he found his mother sitting at her desk having a drink. A gun sat atop the desk. No tranquilizing darts this time.

"For a boy who keeps claiming he wants nothing to do with me, you keep coming back."

"This ends today, Maudette." He was done giving her the title of mother. She'd never earned it.

"I'll end it myself if you go into a whining diatribe of all the ways I've wronged you. Why can't you ever be a man?"

"Argh," he yelled as he threw himself across the room, diving for her desk and scooping the gun. He aimed it at her.

She remained calm in her seat, drink in hand.

"Put that thing down. We both know you don't have the balls to shoot," she said with a sneer. "You're a coward. Like your father."

"Actually, I'm more like you than you think." He pulled the hammer and *click...* Nothing came out of the gun.

His mother laughed. That braying bitchy sound he'd come to hate. "Did you seriously think I'd make it that easy?" She pulled a hidden weapon from her lap. The barrel pointed at him.

"You really going to shoot your own heir?" he said

with a sneer. "Then who would you leave your corrupt empire to?"

"I don't need you, Oliver. The doctors already took what they needed from you to ensure a new generation. I just hope they don't end up disappointments like their father."

The violation, and threat, had him tossing the useless gun to the side and snapping, "Go ahead and shoot me. But don't you dare miss, because I will kill you with my bare hands even if it's the last thing I do."

"No, Ollie. I won't let you." Emma suddenly appeared in the room, and she wasn't empty-handed.

An axe went sailing past him, just missing his mother as she leaned to the side. The glass behind her shattered as the blade struck it.

A chill wind blew into the office, ruffling paper and hair.

His mother stood with her gun and aimed it—at Oliver. "Take one step and I'll kill him."

No surprise his mother thought Emma more precious than him.

"Leave him alone," Emma huffed.

"You are in no position to make demands. Without your horn, you're defenseless."

"Kill him and you'll get nothing from me," Emma spat.

"No one has to die if you both behave." Maudette stalled, meaning she expected reinforcements at any moment. Given he could hear gunfire, he wasn't sure that would happen, but he couldn't afford to wait and find out.

He ran for his mother, whose eyes widened. She fired, the shot hitting him high in the shoulder. He ignored the pain to slam into Maudette, propelling them both out the window.

Emma screamed. "Ollie! No!"

Leaving her was his only regret as the ground rushed to meet him.

Only he never hit it!

He was scooped midair, powerful arms holding him and a familiar voice saying, "Don't panic, I've got you."

Only when he set foot on the ground did he look to see his savior. None other than Adrian. Kind of.

The man appeared like a mishmash of creatures: part lion, eagle with the wings, snake with a tail. A chimera in truth, not just name.

"You saved me."

"Only after you saved us all." Adrian stepped aside, and Oliver could see his mother lying on the ground, her body bent, and yet she still wheezed for breath.

Oliver moved toward her and stood staring down at her. "Why won't you die?" he muttered.

Those blood-red lips split into a smile that was grotesque and triumphant. "I'll never die. I made sure of it."

"What have you done?" he whispered.

Only he never got a reply.

"Your antics end today." Jane stepped into view,

her body covered in a shimmering flame. "Sorry, Oliver, you're about to become an orphan."

Much as he wanted to know what his mother meant, he knew what had to happen.

"End it." He didn't move as Jane stretched out a hand and the body of his mother ignited, the heat so fierce she never had time to scream.

He stood staring at the crackling remains, disgusted by the smell of cooking meat. Kind of hungry, too.

"Ollie!" Emma came flying out of the building and ran for him. He opened his arms wide to catch her and hug her.

It was over. They'd finally rid the world of the one monster that truly counted.

CHAPTER NINETEEN

Adrian took control, looking rather majestic in his beast form. His words emerged guttural, but understandable. "Jayda and Marcus are sweeping the building for more patients. Once they give the all clear, Jane, you know what to do."

"How did you find us?" Oliver asked, keeping his arm tucked around Emma.

"I found out who you were. For some reason, it never came up that you were Maudette Leyghas's son."

"Because I wanted no connection to her. I even changed my name when I began writing to avoid her taint," Oliver said with a shrug.

"Which would have been useful to know before," Jett snapped, having arrived with a glower and a gun in each hand.

"Let's not point fingers here. We've all had something we wanted to hide from in our past," Adrian soothed. "Luckily, I found out, which happened to be about the time Oliver's mother had her mercenaries hit the motel. After that, it was a matter of gathering the team and coming to the rescue. Although it seems you and the others did most of the rescuing yourself."

Oliver hung his head. "This should have never happened. I should have told you from the start my mother had Cerberus and what she planned."

"You're right, you should have. But at least everything ended well. No one was truly injured. It appears we've rescued everyone, except for Xiu, Jacob, and Cerberus. The three of them seem to have vanished."

"Good riddance. Jacob was the one who betrayed us," Emma declared hotly. She wished she'd followed her instinct and gored him when he tried to get rough with her.

"What of Xiu?" Adrian asked.

"We haven't seen her since the attack," Emma stated. Which wasn't surprising given the woman had an uncanny sense about things.

"Since Jacob knows about us and is on the loose, we can't go back to the motel. We'll need to acquire a new safe house." As Adrian spoke, his body and features shifted slowly back, which meant averting her gaze from his naked form until Jett left and returned holding out some clothes.

"I've got the women and children secured in the Suburban. Luke is watching over them," Jett informed. "Any plan on where we should go?"

Oliver stiffened at her side. "Actually, I have the perfect place. We can all stay at my house for now.

Well technically Maudette's, but given she won't be needing it anymore..."

"Does it have a pool?" Jett interrupted.

"Indoor and outdoor," Oliver replied. "Plus a few of the rooms have Jacuzzi tubs."

"And it will already have a security system," Adrian mused aloud. "Sounds like the perfect option. Jett?"

"I'll head over with the gang and make sure it's secure," said Jett.

"You aren't going to shoot the staff, are you?" Oliver asked.

Jett's grin could have rivaled a shark's. "Only if they get in my way."

"Tell them you're my guests. And if they ask about my mother"—Oliver's gaze strayed to the dark and smoldering pile of ash on the concrete—"tell them there was an accident at the lab."

"The wicked witch is dead," Emma murmured. Which meant maybe their nightmare was over.

From the building, Jayda and Marcus emerged at a jog empty-handed.

"Report," Adrian barked.

"Not a single living soul," Jayda said, slowing as she neared. "But lots of blood. Looks like something big with claws went through the lab security team."

Adrian grimaced. "Appears as if your father escaped."

"Given a few of the bodies had bites taken out of

them, I'd say he grabbed a snack for the road. Want me to see if I can track him?" Jayda offered.

Adrian shook his head. "He's probably long gone by now. And we need to get moving before we're noticed and the authorities arrive. Jane, my love, would you do the honors?"

"On it. Although you might want to step away."

The fiery Jane stood before the lab and raised her arms. The flames grew around her, going from a cheerful bright yellow and orange to an intense white hinting of blue and purple. The fire shot from her hands and splashed against the lab, melting through the glass doors at the front, rolling up the building.

In moments, the entire thing burned, removing all the evidence. Incinerating every single secret.

Setting them free.

It was the distant sound of sirens that roused them and got them moving. They piled into the second SUV, Marcus driving with Jayda at his side. Adrian and Jane got the row behind them, whereas Emma and Ollie got the back.

Which was fine. It gave her a chance to use the first aid kit Jayda tossed at her. Ollie didn't say much as she tended the wound in his shoulder. The bullet had gone straight through, and already it had stopped bleeding.

"What happened to you?" she asked as she wrapped his shoulder in gauze. She remembered how he looked when he broke out of his cage.

"Let's just say you and I have more in common

now than really good chemistry in bed." His wry grin brought a ghost of one to her lips.

"I'm sorry, Ollie."

"For what? Not your fault my mother was a psychopath."

"If you hadn't gotten involved with me—"

He shook his head. "Don't you dare take any blame. If I hadn't met you, she still would have injected me. Only I wouldn't have had you to fight for." He stroked a finger down her cheek.

What could she say to that? She snuggled against him.

In less than twenty minutes they pulled past a gate onto a long, winding driveway. They ended up stopped outside a mansion, and Emma gaped.

"Where are we?"

"My house," Ollie said with a sheepish shrug. He hopped out and waited for Emma.

"Um, I can't go in there," she exclaimed when he began tugging her by the hand.

"Why not?"

"Have you seen me?" She glanced down at herself. Her clothing torn and bloody. Her face surely filthy.

"You look beautiful to me."

"You're only saying that so I'll get naked," she huffed.

"Well, duh. Did I mention I have my own private bath? The shower has twelve heads."

"Sounds like a recipe for drowning," she mumbled as he kept tugging her up the steps.

EVE LANGLAIS

The others had no issue with piling out of the vehicles and heading inside. Jett greeted them in the doorway, a twin in the crook of each arm, with Becky hovering close. Luke carried his son—who squealed and clapped his hands, not at all bothered by the horror they'd escaped—on his shoulders.

"Any trouble?" Adrian asked, his arm wrapped around Jane.

"Nothing I couldn't handle," Jett replied.

"Marcus, wanna join me and take a gander at the perimeter?" Jayda asked.

"You should be sure to check out the gazebo by the pond," Oliver shouted as the pair moved off.

As they moved inside, Emma noticed the multi-story foyer with its sweeping staircase. Everything gleamed with cleanliness.

"A place this fancy obviously has servants," she remarked.

"It does, but don't worry. The staff here knows how to be discreet. I assure you, they probably saw much worse while under my mother."

"Yeah, but did they ever see a girl with a horn?" she asked, making sure her hair remained over her forehead, just in case.

"Probably not, but they better get used to it." He grabbed her hand and placed it on his smooth brow. Smooth but for the lump under the skin.

She eyed him in shock. "Oliver! How?"

"Mother, of course. I got a double dose with some

234

of your freshly ground horn today. I'm guessing it's already having an effect."

Adrian noticed them and approached. "What's wrong?"

"Oliver's getting a horn." She wrung her hands in agitation.

"Let me see." Adrian ran his fingers over the lump. "I don't suppose there's a hidden lab in the house."

"Not yet. But tomorrow we can see about getting one set up."

"We'll meet at breakfast, and I'll give you a list." Adrian headed off with Jane to chat with Jett.

Emma hung her head. "I'm so sorry."

"Don't be. This isn't your fault."

"It is, though. My horn infected you."

He snorted. "Still not your fault. I'll handle it."

"But now you'll have to hide, too."

"Or maybe it's time we stopped hiding."

She noticed the use of we. "I thought it was too dangerous."

"Then it's time we changed how the world thinks."

"How?"

"You let me worry about that." He jogged up the stairs, tugging her along by their laced fingers, ignoring their friends who still chattered in the foyer.

"Shouldn't you be showing them around? Giving them rooms?"

"I'm pretty sure they can figure shit out. You're more important."

She was?

The very idea warmed, and she bumped into him. "Still determined to get me naked?"

"Very," he laughed. "But also because you need to wash away what was done to you. Time for you to heal and believe in a better future. A future with me."

"Why, Ollie, are you asking me to go steady with you?" she said with a high-pitched giggle. Excitement at the fact he asked made her giddy.

"I'm asking you to be my everything." He set her down in a bathroom that was finished in gray stone tile. Except for the shower, which was surrounded by clear glass.

She only had eyes for him. She cupped his cheeks. "Why me?"

"Because you're unique and special. Because my heart just about jumps out of my chest when you're around. Because you make my knees weak and my cock hard when I see you. Because you are the one I've been waiting for."

"Oh, Oliver." Then she screeched, "Ollie!" The water hit her backside, chilly for a second before warming and soothing.

His eyes crinkled. "Did I forget to mention the shower is motion activated?"

She slapped him. "I'm all wet."

"Not yet, but you will be." He winked before stepping away, but only so he could divest her of her clothes.

Only when she was nude did he get close enough to claim her mouth. The firm touch of his lips softened her, stoked her arousal. Not that it needed much help. As the hot water sprayed them both, she laced her arms around his neck. His fingers stroked lightly across the skin he'd bared, causing frissons of desire and a heat between her legs that only he could quench.

The patter of hot water relaxed her body and sluiced the filth from her. Washed away the smell of the lab, rinsed away the blood. For once, not blood she'd caused. He made showering into a sensory delight, letting her go only that he might take his soapy hands and lather her flesh with suds. He used the excuse of washing her to intimately explore every inch of her body.

It was enough to make her knees weak. She wobbled, but he was there to hold her up, his arm around her waist, his lips brushing hers with a softly whispered, "Don't fall. We're not done yet."

The very promise in those words had her shivering. He leaned her against the wall, giving her something for support when he got on his knees before her, leaning forward and pressing a kiss on her belly.

Her breath caught, especially as he kept kissing her flesh, his hands on her hips, his mouth so close...oh God so close to where she wanted it.

Her hips arched as desire pulsed in her sex. But did he get the hint?

Nope. He rubbed against her flesh, dragging the rough bristles of his jaw over sensitive skin.

She trembled from head to toe, silently begging for

his mouth to touch her. Instead, he blew on her softly, a hot puff of air on sensitized flesh.

She couldn't help but cry out, and he chuckled, so close she felt the vibration of it, and gasped as a quiver went through her sex.

"My sweet Emma," he whispered against her as his hands spread her thighs.

She tensed in anticipation, but he teased her, kissing the tender skin of her inner thigh, soft butterfly touches up and down, left side then right.

She grabbed hold of his hair and almost demanded he give her what she wanted.

He teased some more, blowing on her, a heated breath that brought a mewling sound past her lips.

"This is mean," she gasped.

"Only if I don't plan to make you come," was his reply. "And you will come. Hard. On my tongue. Won't you, my sweet Emma?"

She almost came at his words. She definitely gushed some honey. She could feel the heat of it pooling in her sex.

He groaned. "You smell so damned good." He finally gave her a lick. Then another. He began lapping at her in quick strokes before he finally placed his mouth on her sex.

She yanked on his hair, her body twitching at the exquisite pleasure of it. And it only got better.

His deft tongue stroked her sex, following the outline of her lips, stabbing at the opening before flicking at her clit.

She might have jerked and bucked against his torturous mouth, but he kept her pinned, holding her in place that he might tease and please.

And, oh, did he ever please. Through heavily lidded eyes she stared down at his head, his hair damp and plastered, her fingers probably tugging too hard, not that he complained.

As if sensing her stare, he paused with his licking, but she didn't mind because his eyes, smoldering with passion, peered up at her and his lips curved into a sensual smile. "Hey, beautiful," he said. "Ready to come for me?"

Was she ever!

His mouth latched onto her clitoris, that most sensitive of nubs. He pulled and tugged on it. Sucked it. Flicked it. Arousal tore through her and brought with it intense pleasure.

But when he thrust two fingers into her, giving her something to clench...

That was when she came, with a cry that was strident and guttural. Her orgasm made her body clench and undulate as she rode his thrusting fingers, melting at his flicking tongue.

When her shudders began to ebb, he withdrew and tugged her with him on legs that wobbled. He wrapped her in fluffy towel and carried her to his bed, laying her on it gently before covering her body with his, his lips latching on for an intense kiss where she could taste herself.

He didn't stay there long. He slid down her body

that he might suck on her nipples, pulling and tugging them into aching peaks while his thigh inserted itself between her legs and rubbed. Rubbed against the core of her, rousing her desire again.

"I want to touch you," she gasped as he bit down on her nipple.

"You touch me, and I'll never make it," he said with a wink.

"What if I'm okay with that?"

He chuckled. "How about I do this instead?" He knelt between her legs, his erection jutting from his body. He stroked his fingers over her nether lips, making her hips jerk and honey pool.

He rubbed the moisture over the head of his cock before positioning himself close enough that the tip brushed her.

She made a noise and arched her hips. The tip of his cock pushed, parting her lips, stretching her, but in a good way. A way that had her breath catching and her body shivering. He took forever to sheath himself, and when he was done, he stayed still within her, pulsing, the fit of him inside so damned tight.

"Fuck me, you feel so damned good." He grunted as he thrust in and out of her. His body glistened with moisture. He grabbed hold of her ass, changing his angle, seating him even deeper inside.

Deep enough he found her sweet spot.

And once he found it, he bumped it over and over. Each stroke drawing a cry. Emma thrashed and clawed at the sheets, meeting his thrusts, her pleasure coiling until she climaxed, her body shaking and shuddering, the experience intense and intimate.

Because for a moment, just a single moment, she felt that connection with Oliver. Felt that moment of perfection where she didn't hear or see but knew, knew in the depths of her soul, that he loved her. Would never hurt her. Would always be there for her.

And that was even better than the amazing sex.

She snuggled against Oliver, forehead to forehead. Not something they could do for long, not with her nub already starting to protrude. But she no longer worried about it coming back.

She'd found acceptance.

Love.

And a man she knew she could count on.

"What are you thinking?" he murmured against her hair, hugging her close.

"I love you."

"Love you, too, Emma. Now and forever."

Together they would face the world. Proudly displaying their horns.

EPILOGUE

THE TRAGEDY THAT ENGULFED THE LAB, LEAVING nothing but soldering ash, was ruled an accident. His mother's remains—what was left on the pavement after she obviously jumped out the window trying to escape the inferno—were DNA matched. Within a few months, the will, making Oliver the only heir, was probated.

With his mother dead, he inherited everything. Including Leyghas Labs, which—while it had lost its main building—still existed. Under Oliver's leadership, he changed the direction of research and mandate, making it about helping those in need rather than profiting—which pissed his shareholders off to no end, until they began seeing mass purchases of their now affordable drugs that brought up volume and profit.

Oliver funded new hospitals for the severely injured, investing in state-of-the-art prosthetic labs and the most skilled technicians.

He hired the best doctors he could find, including an unknown relative called Adrian Chimera, who found a treatment for cancer that was better than chemo. He was written up in a few medical journals but declined any awards or spotlight, claiming he owed a debt to humanity.

And the world ate up his modesty, much to Jett's amusement.

In the end, a lot of good came of the Chimera Secrets, and no more monsters. Not intentionally created ones at any rate. While Oliver had come around to agreeing that Chimera had done some good, he couldn't condone the continuation.

Which was why it was good Adrian realized, on his own, "I don't have the right to change people without permission."

As for those that were already and forever different?

Those that survived ended up banding together. Given Oliver now had a horn, much like Emma's, he stayed out of the limelight as much as possible. The times he did have to leave meant shearing the nub and wearing a low-brow hat. He learned to live with bangs, but hated them.

He didn't leave home often. The estate he bought in Wyoming helped with that privacy. By the time he was done shopping for property, he practically owned an entire town and the land around it. Over one hundred thousand acres and he kept it protected.

Cameras were dotted all over the place, and the

few roads leading into the area watched everyone who entered. What the eyes in the sky could see was controlled by Marcus and his state-of-the-art computer room—which Jayda more than teased made him hornier than her Trekkie uniform.

The town itself had a high-tech police force—overseen by Jayda, who laughed when Adrian presented her with a uniform.

"Me, a fucking cop?" she'd joked. But she took the job. It gave her the authority she needed to keep an eye on outsiders and make sure everyone toed the line, because, lo and behold, a few of the missing Chimera Secrets somehow found their way.

Jett and Luke provided personal security for their more vulnerable inhabitants. Not that the children needed much protection. Part of their education was about teaching them how to blend in and defend themselves. Because out of sight of the world, and flourishing in the compound, all of Chimera's secrets gathered, along with a few that wandered into town, different and afraid, also strange because they didn't come out of any science lab. But theirs was a story for another day.

Left alone, those who started out as Chimera Secrets multiplied, many choosing to pair with a human who accepted their secret, their children usually inheriting a special trait. They grew faster than their human counterparts, which meant they'd enter the world as adults within a decade at the most. Mingling with the population. Seeding their evolution subtly. They'd need those numbers. Would need to be strong, because, one day soon, a war would be coming.

The devil, formerly known as Dr. Cerberus, had reappeared only once after his escape from the lab. And on a video uploaded to *YouTube* of all things.

His yellow-eyed gaze had stared into the camera, and he'd smiled—a terrible thing with seeping smoke— as he said, "Soon the age of man will come to an end, giving rise to the era of monsters. My monsters. My legions."

And when it happened, the next generation, born in secret, would be there to fight them.

THE END.

LOOKING FOR MORE STORIES? VISIT EVELANGLAIS.COM

CPSIA information can be obtained
at www.ICGtesting.com
Printed in the USA
BVHW030208161219
566802BV00001B/158/P